ADAM

ADAM

Shelby Wratchford

ISBN (paperback): 9781737076902
ISBN (ebook): 9781737076919

Set in 11-point Baskerville

Cover design by Shelby Wratchford

Library of Congress Control Number: 2021907684

Printed in the United States of America

First Paperback Edition, 2021

Publisher's Cataloging-in-Publication Data
Names: Wratchford, Shelby, 1996- author.
Title: Adam / Shelby Wratchford.
Description: First paperback edition. | Fults : Shelby Wratchford, [2021]
Identifiers: ISBN: 978-1-7370769-0-2 (paperback) | 978-1-7370769-1-9 (ebook) | LCCN: 2021907684
Subjects: LCSH: Technology and state—Social aspects—Fiction. | Totalitarianism—Fiction. | Control (Psychology)—Fiction. | Social justice—Fiction. | End of the world—Fiction. | Judgement Day—Fiction. | Rescue work—Fiction. | Death—Fiction. | Grief—Fiction. | Loss (Psychology)—Fiction. | Despair—Fiction. | Man-woman relationships—Fiction. | LCGFT: Dystopian fiction. | Science Fiction. | Apocalyptic fiction. | Romance fiction. | Political fiction. | Psychological fiction. | BISAC: FICTION / Science Fiction / Apocalyptic & Post-Apocalyptic. | FICTION / Dystopian. | FICTION / Science Fiction / General.
Classification: LCC: PS3623.R383 A33 2021 | DDC : 813/.6—dc23

But you can't make people listen. They have to
come 'round in their own time, wondering what
happened and why the world blew up under them.
It can't last.

RAY BRADBURY, FAHRENHEIT 451

CHAPTER 1

"13,000 deaths, that's what I heard."

"13,000 already?"

"I thought there would have been more by now."

I watched the two men talking like it was nothing, like it didn't matter. 13,000 people dead and counting, and to them, it was just another story on the news. It was nothing. They were numb to it, just like everyone else here. Just like everyone everywhere.

"Get up, and don't make me tell you again. Who do you think is going to clean those tables?"

"Sure, Linda." I breathed out slowly and exasperatedly just to get under her skin even further.

She rolled her eyes. "What am I even paying you for?" she mumbled, half sarcastically and half seriously, as she disappeared behind me into the kitchen, and I was left sitting at the bar with a damp cloth slung over one shoulder.

"I hear Cincinnati is trying to get the people to evacuate," one of the men said to the other.

"I don't believe it. Any of it," said the other one casually, indifferently detached. "It's all just another news headline," he murmured, knocking back another shot of brandy.

All the while they spoke to one another, they never took their eyes off the Screen that took up most of the room and projected outward toward the customers. They never looked at one another, none of them. It was just the Screens. It was always the Screens. Everywhere you looked. The only break from it was when you were working, and even then, you might be like me, catching glimpses of the distraction or receiving the inputs directly to the brain through a Monitor, a small chip implant in the back of the skull that acted as a one-stop shop for all media and communication needs.

As I thought about what the man said, it bothered me more and more. Just another "news" headline. Most reports weren't even news anymore; they were made up. Maybe the most recent installation was just another action-packed drama to distract us from the reality of our declining social structure, privacy, and freedom, if they could even be considered applicable to our condition. A distraction would make sense, but the media was putting a lot of effort into it if that was the case.

Three weeks ago, that was when I first saw the headlines or heard them, rather. I was working the late shift at the time, finishing up when a loud buzzer sounded throughout the entire country and the rest of the land that made up the Regime, or what used to be individual "states." But that was just another urban legend. The education system didn't teach us history. Too dangerous. Just look to the future; that was the underlying theme for all of it. In fact, the people employed in the past to help us understand our world and our place in it, or merely their biased opinions of both, didn't teach us at all anymore. That was also the job of the Monitors.

"Red zone: Cincinnati" flashed across the large televised Screen as I was mopping up spilled beer that night. There followed a long broadcast and images of what looked like a deep crack that had emerged from an aggravated earthquake site. That was nothing new. Definitely not newsworthy, for similar chaos erupted pretty much every day. Some natural disaster was always striking, and they'd become progressively worse since the San Andreas incident when a good portion of the West Coast was sucked right into the mantle and filled up with dirty brown ocean water like it was never there. People were afraid we were all just going to break off and disappear, but the devastation wasn't too bad in hindsight. Nothing like World War IV. Half the population died during the nuclear holocaust, but it was a catastrophe mended by technology. There was nothing machines couldn't fix. And voila, a thousand babies were born. But that was normal. Machines were much better at genetics and disease prevention than we ever were.

The media televised the works. The blood, the dead, the dying, the fires, the government's meek attempt to control it, and the Head of Regime giving a most deeply unfelt message to the starving masses of Cincinnati. And they ate it up, even as their families bled to death around them. They believed every broken and idiotic word that was spoken. They believed that it would be fixed in no time and that their pain and suffering would bring recompense. They believed that there was something we could do. But it couldn't be controlled; it was nature. Even with all of our "superior" knowledge, we couldn't control the weather. Scientists threw up chemicals and protective balances into the sky, but it still stormed. All the Dome kept out was the acidic rain and radiation. It had prevented natural disasters before, but what about now? Fires were destroying Cincinnati, and that earthquake . . . It was just a matter of time before the Earth split under our feet.

The Regime refused to let anyone with a Monitor believe that, though. The Dome was built to protect us. We were going to be okay. But the Dome was just a byproduct of the war, along with growing dissent against the country, fear of nuclear fallout, fear of losing more lives, and the government, in turn, fearing there would be no one left to control. People wanted freedom, but they no longer knew what that was, and machines made our lives easier. They made people feel safe again, and so did the Dome.

When it was first built, people were still allowed to leave. But that quickly changed after a massive pandemic swept through the population still recovering from World War IV. Now, only those on official government business were allowed to leave, and if you were lucky—or delusional, depending on your viewpoint—enough to manage to escape, there was nothing waiting for you on the outside but a wasteland and absolute starvation, thanks to the eradication of almost all wildlife outside the walls of the Dome. Inside, everything was monitored and controlled, from the wildlife to the food to where you lived to your income and everything in between. Evolution no longer had a say, and neither did the people the Dome was built to protect. But that was just hearsay if you asked the Regime.

The Dome covered almost the entire country, save New Anchorage, the offshore holding, and it reached from Las Vegas on the western border to Pittsburg on the eastern. It was supposed to shield us from the continually rising water levels that had already taken a good portion of the areas directly bordering the oceans, another devastation like that of San Andreas, the acidity in the rain, and the radiation, but there were people—people like me—that didn't fully believe all of it. The Dome could shield us to some extent; it had proven itself capable of that in the past. It could produce a force shield that extended about a mile outside of it to deter water from coming anywhere close, and if that didn't work, it could raise a metal barrier that reached several hundred feet into the air, tall enough to withstand the average tsunami. It also regulated temperatures within, meaning the wildfires, tropical storms, and droughts that continuously threatened the world outside the Dome only affected those of us under it to a minuscule fraction of that degree, and any temperature-related disasters like forest fires inside the Dome were usually caused by humans and quickly shut down by scientists.

Still, if anything happened to the electrical system that made up the Dome, if it failed, then so would the protection. The Dome was a brilliant technological feat, but it was also delicate and had only been around for about one hundred years in its current state. It was far from foolproof, and people like me believed there were other ways to protect ourselves. To adapt.

The Regime built the Dome to keep us in and keep everyone else out. There was nothing more to it.

And now the natural disasters were happening inside, not out. We were trapped.

Yet, nobody cared.

The broadcast from Cincinnati the men spoke of was just another source of numb entertainment. Like it was a movie, not reality. There was no real danger. Nobody was fazed by the images of people being sucked into the crack and buried alive under fallen buildings, or the man burning to death because of a power line that snapped due to the ruptured fault, as they were calling it unofficially. Officially it was "nothing to worry about," like the old man at the table said. The people they showed on the Screens probably did what they did to get on the air. Probably drove their autonomes straight into the crack, and then their families were paid a pretty penny for the sacrifice. And anyone would do anything for the money. Who could blame them, though? Live or starve. They didn't understand. 13,000 people were dead. 13,000 and counting.

CHAPTER 2

"Adam Krichmar, please," the robotic voice sounded, radiating throughout the building but not heard above the roar of advertisement Screens in bright, eye-catching colors.

"Adam Krichmar, please report to the identification desk."

I rolled my eyes as a machine stabbed my finger and processed my DNA.

Fingerprints were hacked around the time of the Depression, which occurred somewhere between the recession and the war between the Regime and a country that started with a "c," possibly. During that time, vagabonds tapped into the system and could cross borders into different regions of the Regime without being persecuted, which ended in the deaths of a number of people whose identities had been stolen and the eventual euthanizing of the criminals.

After the machine confirmed my DNA identification, I was shoved toward a retinal scanner, then a full-body x-ray before I was even allowed to set foot on the train. Even then, I was stopped. A person who looked more machine than man held his arm out as I moved to step into the craft, the Tram, hovering above the blue-streaked electric panels that guided it.

"State your purpose."

"Just a quick trip for leisure."

The man stared at me, or at least I took him to be staring

at me. I couldn't see his face behind the all-black, full-body armored suit and helmet. "I've seen you at the Border before . . ." He paused. When they paused, that meant they were searching. They could see every record of every person. Where they were born, where they went to school, where they worked. Their blood type, their history, their disturbance records, their family, and all the surveillance that had ever been recorded of them. That didn't give people a good chance of getting away with criminal conduct, which was exactly what the security personnel wanted. I didn't have a reason to leave the city for one in another region, but I did so because I needed to get away from the memories that haunted me in Vegas. I saved up the money I made at the bar to take low-class Trams to different areas every so often. Apparently, that was a red flag.

I stared at the man dead on during the suspended silence between us, though there was never any real silence. The faint buzz of the Monitors was always nearby.

"You visit the Border often, Krichmar?" he asked me, his tone neither questioning, demanding, or angry. It was just there. No emotion. "Do you?" he repeated just as indifferently as before.

"Sometimes," I admitted, secure in the fact that I had nothing to hide from the man. At least, not in that regard. "Sometimes you have to disappear." It wasn't an answer I should've given, but I didn't want to lie. I hoped he could relate.

Whether he did or not, I never found out, but his arm eventually fell to his side, and he scanned my identification chip for my pass. I let out a breath of the hot, sticky Las Vegas air when I finally stepped onto the Tram. Sometimes I took it to the Edge to get away, or disappear, as I said. Though, even inside the Tram, traveling away from the consistent screaming and bombardment of capital stimulus devouring the city—devouring everything under the Dome—Screens lined the inside of the machines, and I still heard the faint buzzing noise of a Monitor. I glanced at the source of the hum: a man across the aisle whose eyelids were closed in sleep but whose hands typed quickly on a synthesized keyboard in his lap. There was nowhere you could go to truly be alone. There was always someone nearby, and there was always a Monitor.

I originally planned to take the five-minute train ride from Las Vegas to St. Louis, the capital of the Regime, before realizing I had little time before my next shift at the bar. I decided to take the Tram to the Edge instead. It was just outside the city where the ocean came close enough to the Dome for us to see without ever leaving its protection. That would have to be good enough this time.

When we stopped at the small station, I got off with the others: the low-class or "squatter," as some called us, though we were nowhere near the Untouchables, who weren't allowed to use the Trams. You had to be a citizen to do so.

I departed and watched as some elites from other Trams bought additional passes; easy enough as you only had to think how you wanted it, and the Monitor confirmed available funds and transferred it to the correct station. Some boarded Trams taking scenic routes around the Regime, and I wondered what it would be like to have money to travel like that. When I did, it was only ever for a few hours, at most, and the low-class Trams never took the scenic routes.

I stepped out of the station and frowned. This was the most scenic it got for me: a littered beach that was so polluted, the water was more brown than blue, and plastic waste floated in piles on its surface. Even if you somehow managed to get outside the Dome, the water would be impossible to swim in.

I looked back at some of the others who'd been on the Tram with me. Some hadn't even come outside. Why experience the sand and the salty air when you could just watch it from the window of the Tram above?

In Vegas, some never even made it onto the Tram in the first place, too numb to move and standing there at the platform until someone either shoved their miserable bodies onto the tracks or else Border Control took them in under "examination." Depression was a sign of a defective Monitor.

A person could undergo surgery to have it replaced, but they'd most likely end up dead. Some, like me, found a way to continue. It was hard, and it took time. We were always under surveillance, always, and there were always machines watching for someone like me: a low-class bartender trying to make the most of the system we were forced into. I wanted to see more. Was that such a crime? I dreamed of visiting the East Coast one day, or maybe somewhere north, but I knew I'd never have the money.

I left after a few minutes.

"Watch it." A man, not much older than myself, maybe in his mid-twenties, shoved past me as I exited the Tram back at the Vegas station, knocking my body forward into another, slightly older man. He looked at me disgustedly. He wore a grey, fitted suit and appeared to be heading to a Tram destined for the Capital. He used his shoulder to push me back, and I nearly hit a woman standing close behind me in the crowded station. There were so many of us.

I looked back at the dazed woman. Her eyes were unblinking. She looked like the kind that had given up. She'd get knocked onto the tracks; I was sure of that. I would've been the one to do it if I hadn't seen her. I now noticed how close we both were to the tracks. How close all of us adhered to them. The two of us were only inches away from instant death by electrocution. That possibility existed for all of us, and it did happen. The news also used to televise that, but we'd seen it a thousand times over by now. No longer entertainment.

The whirl of the fast-paced traffic around the old woman and me mimicked my fast-beating heart. I looked around and caught sight of one of the guards; he, too, looked like a machine. He watched us for a minute, then pointed a long, black-gloved finger at the still woman behind me. Another guard came up next to the man and nodded his head. Her Monitor was defective. That was the only explanation for her behavior.

You can't leave her, Adam, a voice in my head told me. My voice. I turned to face her and could see, as she turned her head slightly to the side, the raised scar that started behind her ear and disappeared into her hair. It was from the earpiece that attached to the implanted Monitor and was needed to hear the signals the computer received.

The Monitors took away one's thoughts. Experts said they interacted with people, guided them away from danger, protected them, and helped them "overcome" their fears and misunderstandings. That was a lie. A Monitor became one's thoughts and feelings. It became everything, eventually, depending on how susceptible or not a person was to the constancy of the stimulus. But the people who developed them didn't tell consumers that; they just shoved it down our throats, promising only positive benefits. One had to find out the hard way what the reality of the chip was, and then it was too late. The person was already gone. Scientists had cured cancer. The deadliest disease became one of metal and wires, not cells.

This woman will die. The thought entered the back of my mind. She stood out from the crowd. Everyone else around us was a blur, just vacant faces in the mass, with the occasional glare when one accidentally ran into the other, or when one of the high-class professionals had the tasking job of naming off their intents at the Border. How could they be asked such a thing? I wished they could see themselves from my point of view and see how truly detached and inhuman they'd become. They didn't care. It didn't faze them that the woman standing before me, that living, breathing human, would be taken away because of her mental state. She was going to be killed, but they didn't pay attention. It wouldn't matter if she were jostled onto the tracks by the bolstering crowd to have her face melted off or if she committed suicide out of hopeless vacancy. They wouldn't care if she took out a gun right here, right this second, and shot herself. We'd seen it a thousand times over. We were accustomed to gore. We merely shrugged our shoulders or didn't do anything at all. It was nothing new. Society taught us not to feel. If we did, we hurt, we feared, and we didn't perform.

I snapped back to my senses with an alarming jolt of realization. I could think about how wrong it was for as long as I wanted, but what was that going to change in the end?

You can't let her die. You can't let that happen.

I moved toward her. "Are you—" I began, but her arm shot out instantly, stopping me from taking another step.

"No," she half whispered, half choked, her hand pressed weakly against my chest. "No, they'll take you too." She stared at me. Her glossy eyes were bloodshot and encircled by sunken in, grey-blue sockets, and her skin was too tightly stretched from old cosmetic enhancements. The surgeries never lasted; eventually, we all aged.

Despite her attempts to prevent the inevitable, the woman had grown old, though it looked more as if the life had been sucked out of her. Her frail stature wasn't natural. If I took a breath, it might break every bone in her tiny, shrunken body.

"Please." She coughed, still staring at me with her wide, glazed eyes. I couldn't tell if she was looking at me or off somewhere in the distance. "They'll see you." I knew she was talking about the guards.

"And what if they do?" I said, slightly confused at her resistance to my help.

"It's alright," she said slowly under her breath. She would not meet my eyes, and it seemed as if she was talking to herself. "Too young, too young." Some people would say she was crazy. I knew it wasn't her fault.

"You don't know . . ." She looked at me finally. Her bony hand clenched my shoulder, and her sharp, pointed nails dug deep into my skin. I winced but didn't move. She looked fearful, though purposed. "It's no use," she murmured, and her whole body trembled. "Cincinnati," she said breathlessly. "The news."

I nodded my head tentatively at this, waiting for the point. I was beginning to worry there might not be one. I'd grown all too familiar with the way she acted. It was how my mother was sometimes. The Monitors did that to people: made them talk nonsense.

"Judgment," she whispered in a croaking voice. I was beyond confused, and I must have given her that look. "He's watching us now," she explained.

"Who?" I asked, my anxiety escalating. I was acutely aware of the man that looked like a machine coming toward us. "Who's watching?"

She looked around the place. "The guard?" I asked, trying to get an answer. It reminded me how much I hated being patient. What annoyed me further was my own frustration. And the buzzing of the Monitor. It surrounded her.

"No guard." She tilted her heavy head from side to side, and it rocked like nothing was holding it up. "He's watching," she repeated, finally pointing a shaky finger upwards. I followed her line of sight. The clear dome was above us, blocking out the acid rain, wind, and harsh UV rays that the ozone no longer could. That wasn't what she wanted me to see, was it?

Her eyes dropped down as I returned my gaze to her meek face. Her expression was satisfied, as though she'd done what she needed to. Like that had been her whole purpose. That was insane and didn't make any sense. There had to be more. I wanted to ask her, but my ignorance held me back. What use was it? She was already gone.

But it matters, Adam.

"Who are you?" I asked her, but she wouldn't look at me. I repeated the question, and then again three times before she motioned behind her. The guard in the black suit was moving closer.

"Go," she said.

That was the last thing she ever said. Then she was gone. Her body fell onto the tracks, vanishing with nothing but the pop of her electrified Monitor faint against the noise of the machines, and a singeing smell that found its way to me. An incoming Tram quickly blew past, taking everything with it. Nobody saw. Nobody cared.

I let myself realize for a moment that she'd saved me. It wasn't normal for people to stand around in stations like we just had. She would've been deemed mentally unstable, and I didn't want to think about what would've happened to me. She'd distracted the guards, and the surveillance cameras were turned to the tracks the moment her body hit them. Another death for the records, and it meant that the agents were distracted, if only for a few minutes. They needed to account for her death.

Because of the woman's actions, I had the chance to leave the station without being questioned by security, though my body felt frozen from shock. I couldn't believe that she threw herself onto the tracks and ended her own life in a matter of seconds. Had she been planning that? Had she really been standing there in the first place? It took every ounce of will inside me to make my feet move toward the exit of the building.

Go, Adam. Now. Before they detain you.

I was a witness to a suicide. I was the last person that spoke to her before she died. Security would ask me questions about her actions and what she said, and if they started questioning me, there was the chance they'd uncover the truth about Adam Krichmar.

CHAPTER 3

"Excuse me."

"Sorry."

"Excuse me."

I shoved my way through the thick marching mass of commuters. Rush hour. Glares and angry hissing sneers were thrown my way. They only traveled north and south. No one ever deviated. I'm moving this way; you're moving that way. Don't touch me; I won't touch you. Don't look at me; I won't look at you. We were just passersby. It was an unspoken pact between us all. I probably seemed like an alien, traveling straight through their moving mass of one way or the other. I could hear the incessant buzzing engulfing me as I moved, rushing in and out and all around me.

"Excuse me," I said, only to receive yet another bewildered stare. Why didn't I just keep my mouth shut and my head down like I knew I should? I was trying not to draw attention to myself after all. I knew this. I also knew why I spoke out loud. I needed to hear myself speak, to know and keep reminding myself that I was really here. I was afraid I might lose myself in the ceaseless hum. I was afraid I'd become the woman that had been standing right in front of me only moments ago.

Her shuddering, lifeless figure formed before my eyes. Her skin stretched taught over her face like a mask. Everything about her seemed artificial. But she'd been there: that was real. She'd been alive, then she was gone, and no one noticed. It was terrifying, but no one cared. In an instant, the image in my mind of her standing before me turned into a figure of melted skin, burnt hair, and wires. The smell of metal and burning flesh still permeated the air, but no one took notice of that either. A few people wrinkled their noses, but that was it. I did, though. My mouth fell open as I imagined the tracks and the exposed muscles on the woman's body. I imagined the wires all over her: around her neck, weaving out of the orbits of her eyes, slowly snaking down her esophagus and into her stomach. It was replacing her: the Monitor.

"Woah!" I grunted as the force of my moving body collided with another, and the image of the woman evaporated. I'd run into a girl slightly younger than me. "Sorry, sorry," I mumbled as I quickly knelt to gather the small bag that had fallen as I'd crashed into her. She reached out slowly, never saying a word, and took the bag back.

"I'm sorry, I wasn't watching where I was going," I apologized again.

Just shut up, I thought vaguely. She probably couldn't even hear what I was saying above the roar surrounding us.

I realized after a moment just how familiar this girl looked, but I couldn't be sure of where I'd seen her before. Maybe a face in a magazine that hers was copied from. But her face didn't look "enhanced," or maimed rather, though the signs of that were hard to distinguish, even by most professionals, at her age. You could be anyone if you had the money. It all took money, so I was stuck with my own miserable self. Some part of me liked that I was.

Why wasn't she moving? "I'm sorry," I began hopelessly again.

Just move, Adam. You can't be seen. The guards will see you. They'll stop you. Then what? I'd done nothing wrong, but they might blame me for what happened to the woman. I'd been standing right next to her before she threw herself onto the tracks.

I glanced around the room nervously. The security agents

I noticed earlier were near the tracks, making sure people stood far enough away from them so the same thing didn't happen twice this afternoon. That would only last so long; my clock was ticking, but I couldn't move.

The girl was staring at me. I wanted to watch her all day; she was beautiful. But it wasn't right. She just stood there, her gaze fixed on me, unlike the others. I didn't know what to do. Her eyes weren't glazed over. I could plainly hear she had a Monitor, but that didn't seem to be the reason she wouldn't move. She wasn't lost, not like the woman. The image of her body on the tracks began to creep its way back into my mind, but I shook it away, concentrating on the girl in front of me. For a moment, I thought I was hallucinating and had the overwhelming urge to reach out and touch her to make sure she was real but couldn't bring myself to do the simple enough task. I couldn't bring myself to touch her. Physical touch wasn't exactly accepted among strangers or anyone for that matter. Too risky, really.

The girl was studying me; that had to be it. Was she? She didn't wear the iconic black helmet of the men who were more like machines. Maybe she had a Lens; you couldn't see those, after all.

Come on, Adam. What are you doing? I began to twitch slightly under discomfort and the awkwardness of the situation. The buzzing was ringing all around me and growing louder the longer I stood still, my heart racing. A few people gave us odd looks, adding to my stress, though most didn't care enough to pay attention.

Even if they didn't care, I did. I couldn't get caught, and the agents were already dispersing back into the crowd.

It's been too long. Go, now!

I turned around, fighting every screaming internal urge to stay, to wait for a response, or anything for that matter, from the girl. But I turned and left the station as fast as I could, focusing on the buzzing to take my mind off her. I let the noise engulf me and numb me to the point where I could no longer think. And I walked. Past the heart of the city, to the surrounding poverty-stricken shithole that I called home. As long as I didn't think, I was okay. It hurt to think, to feel. Was I heading in the same direction as the old woman?

CHAPTER 4

I rolled around on the lump of a couch in my deteriorated apartment—if that's what you could call the one-room place with nothing but the couch and a way to keep a little food—and listened with wide eyes to the tick of the clock marking the slowly passing time. The three-dimensional images of the city made their way through the grime-covered windows and danced on the yellowed walls of my apartment. After a while, I no longer noticed them and began to see things that were not truly there.

I dreamt of my mother with my eyes open. The images were so bright, so vivid, so clear. I tried to drown them out with the ads from the Screens, the roar of the engines, the click of the electric sockets, and the faint moan of the Monitors, though there weren't as many of those in my neighborhood as there were elsewhere. Untouchables lived in the abandoned buildings not far away.

I tried to focus on the surrounding noise, but I couldn't erase my mother. She was beautiful and exactly as I remembered her from my childhood, though that image of her didn't last long. Slowly, she morphed into the old woman who'd killed herself on the tracks, taking her own life, much like my mother had. I watched it happen over and over again in my mind, an outsider looking in on the moment I had tried to block out forever. I saw myself open the door to her room.

I watched her in the moments before she took her life: helpless, afraid, and confused.

I saw her stand by the window and watched her ignore me when I called her name to ask what was wrong. I watched her look at me like she was trying to memorize my every feature. I saw her put the barrel to her head and saw myself do absolutely nothing. I heard the trigger pull and the crash of her lifeless body that followed. There was so much blood . . . The last thing I heard was the sound of my feet as I ran.

Only the elite could hold ceremonies anymore for the dead. We still celebrated the ones we loved, but there wasn't room for everyone in the cemeteries. The rest of us just dealt with the forced arrangements or didn't. I was a boy who ran away and never had the chance to see what became of the body of the woman that gave me life. Her ashes might've become a part of the earth, spread on a hillside, or mixed with trash in a dump if her body was even burned. I'd never know. She was only a part of me by memory; her name erased from my birth certificate and replaced with another. I had denied her death for so long and tried to forget her for even longer.

I jolted upright, my heart pounding as if I was still running, and sat on the tattered couch breathing heavily. My mind slowly drifted to the girl. I ran from her at the Border Station as I'd run from my mother after her suicide.

I lied earlier when I said I was glad I was stuck with myself. I was just like the rest. On my own miserable quest to unfeeling silence. I'd like to have blamed my mother for all my problems, but she took her life to save mine. I didn't have anyone to blame but myself for my outlook.

I threw the dirty glass bottle filled with muddy brown drinking water sitting on the table nearby and watched it hit the wall with a loud crash. The polluted water momentarily covered the bright colors of the ads streaming through the windows from the Screens covering the buildings on the outskirts of the city, but the ads would never go away. Never.

I got up and took some sleeping pills, then lay back down and waited to drift into another world. But I never escaped reality or my memories, no matter how hard I tried. Maybe I was losing my mind and heading in the same direction as my mother, the woman from the tracks, and, really, all of us.

I just happened not to have a Monitor infecting me directly. Yet.

That's right; you don't. You have freedom, Adam. You can make your own choices. I could make my own choices without the influence of a Monitor directly, but I constantly lived in fear of being discovered. That was the reason I ran from the station. I wanted to bang my head against the wall for not having done anything when I was there. I could've stopped the old woman from killing herself, even though she probably would have sooner or later. If not that, I could've taken the opportunity that she presented me with. As horrible as it was, she was a distraction for the security agents. I could've slipped onto a Tram headed for a different region. It didn't matter where the Tram was going, as long as it was far away from Vegas. There were too many painful memories from the city, the place where my mother died. Anywhere was better than where I grew up.

I could've gotten out, but I'd run from that possibility instead, right into that girl—the girl whose name I didn't even know. She seemed familiar, and it frustrated me that I couldn't figure out how I knew her. I wished more than anything that I did. Out of a billion people in the crowd, she was the one I'd run into.

The thought was ridiculous. No, it was fucking insane. But maybe it was for a reason?

No. Shut up, Adam. Coincidence did not equal fate. And what was fate after all? Our world was doomed, and if fate was to thank, then I did not want to be involved with it in the least.

I lay on the dilapidated couch, rolling over these useless thoughts, forgetting completely what the woman at the station said to me. Was it just a delusional trance she'd been in, or did her words have some importance? I remembered the way she'd pointed insistently at the sky. All that was above us was the Dome, but she wanted me to see something beyond that.

"He's watching . . ." Her words whirled in my head, but I didn't understand them.

I pictured myself in grade school, sitting at a desk surrounded by other children in ratty clothes with dirt and sweat smeared across them as we stared at a Screen. It told us about something called faith. There was another word. It started with an "r." It took me a minute, and then I remembered the word was "religion." It held a lot of meaning to people before the Regime. To me, it meant nothing at all, but I recalled how the Screen talked about people who watched over us. They weren't exactly people; they were much more powerful, or thought to be at one point in history. There were certain religions, if I wasn't wrong, where there was a single being that held power over everything else. I didn't remember the name, but it was important, or so we were told. Like I said, we weren't taught much about the past, and who knew what of it was true, but the few things we were told about were only to show us how bad the world used to be. Our teachers tried to show us why the way we lived was so much better, in their eyes—or the eyes of those controlling the education system. And when rhetoric is shoved down your throat your entire life, when it's the only thing you know, it becomes the truth.

They only taught us about "religion" because it was at the root of humanity's problems for thousands of years. People died for it. People were slaughtered—quartered and burnt alive—because of it. People couldn't be who they wanted to be because of it. It gave people an excuse to blindly destroy great works of art, entire cities, civilizations, and ethnicities, and it was the cause of all ancient wars and conflicts.

As a kid, it terrified me. But now? It seemed like we'd just replaced one giant problem with another.

I thought about it for a few more minutes, then drifted back to thinking about my mother and the woman. Too many people died and were forgotten about so easily. The people in Cincinnati were losing their lives, and for what?

And what was I doing? If I stayed here, I'd wind up just

like them.

I made up my mind. First, I would have to find the girl. She was there only moments after the old woman killed herself. Two people deviating from the crowd and acting strange in a short period of time. That couldn't be a coincidence. I rarely ever met people that deviated, let alone two people in one day. Second, I would have to get beyond the Border. Beyond the boundary of the Dome. There had to be more to life than what I was experiencing. If I stayed, I knew I'd lose myself entirely.

CHAPTER 5

"Adam, you can't keep moping around like this. It isn't right," I said aloud only for myself to hear. I kicked the leg of one of the bar stool chairs forward and grabbed it to heave it onto the counter. Linda was gone, and it was just me for the night, and naturally, I decided to close at ten o'clock. That was extremely early by our standards, for a bar or anything, considering the fact that almost every business offered twenty-four-hour service to maximize revenue. If you wanted to compete in this world, you had to. There was also the fact that most people didn't sleep. How could anyone with the constancy of the Screens and their ads? And who needed to sleep when we could just take a pill to keep ourselves awake? Of course, it was biologically necessary to sleep at least a few hours every once and a while, so the Monitors would allow our brains to believe we were sleeping while keeping the rest of us fully functional and operating on a preprogrammed list of to-dos. Or, you were an insomniac like me.

The bags were puffy and discolored under my eyes in the reflection of the black Screen in front of me. It shut down automatically when I entered "closing" into the building's system, which then sent signals to the Monitors and made most people remaining at the bar leave. I had to handle the ones who didn't have Monitors myself, though they generally didn't make themselves known. They tended to get up and leave when those with Monitors did.

Monitors were endorsed—enforced might be a better word—by the government, and almost everyone everywhere in the Regime had one. They started out as a sign of wealth and privilege and were marketed as something that we all needed. But now, they were normal. They made our lives easier. They made our lives better. Anything outside of that was considered criminal. If you were someone who didn't have one, like me, you had to keep that fact hidden.

All in all, the customers didn't seem to mind my decision to close too terribly. They griped for a moment, then found another place and another Screen. There was always one around wherever.

As I finished closing and wiping down the counter, I toyed with the idea of returning to the Border. Reality had quelled my determination of the night before, but it didn't stop the images and thoughts that crept their way into my mind. All day, I kept thinking about the old woman and how quickly she'd disappeared from the world. How quickly she'd taken her own life. Just like my mother.

Then I pictured the girl. She was so beautiful. And I watched as she either threw herself onto the tracks or put a gun to her head. I kept having these horrible visions of her pulling the trigger and exposing a mass of wires where her brain had been.

The sounds of the Monitors rang in my ears louder and louder as the day went by, and I started to imagine everyone faceless, nothing but wires left underneath.

I had to stop myself from screaming; the images were so overwhelming. No one would've heard me anyway. Even before the customers left, I doubted they would've cared.

Now, the place was sealed shut. The only things I could see were the images and adverts pouring in from outside the large glass windows at the front entrance of the bar. I spoke aloud to myself, needing to hear my name. I needed to hear something besides the deafening messages of the ads.

"Lip enhancements, only $500 at Mel's Beauty . . ."

"Free pass to the tracks after signing up for clinical trials, call 1-800-991-3645 . . ."

And on, and on . . .

"Just breathe, Adam."

I let out a sigh as I hunched forward at the bar, my arms propping up my head. So tired. I needed to close my eyes. It had been a long day with no breaks, and my mind still ached from the night before. I needed to sleep: something I was lacking immensely.

My eyes were half closed, and my thoughts were finally fading. All that remained was the girl's image. I needed to know, had to know why she'd stopped. Why had she looked at me, unlike everyone else who just kept walking? No one cared, but she'd stopped. I was convinced that I was going insane. It must have been a lapse in her Monitor that made her freeze before me . . . But she'd looked me in the eyes, hadn't she? There was something besides the Monitor there. There had to have been. I wasn't the only person left in the world who still thought for myself. I knew I wasn't. There were people, vagabonds I called them, out there.

I sat at the counter and drifted asleep while I thought of her. There was one resolution clear and final on my mind: the Border. Tomorrow. I was grasping at straws. Escape wasn't possible. I knew that would take time, but I didn't want to wait any longer. I would take my meager savings and buy a pass somewhere far away. I'd figure it out once I was there, right? Above all else, I desperately hoped to see the girl again.

CHAPTER 6

It was already on the news. Everything was in chaos when I awoke, jerked from sleep by the shrieking of sirens and warning signals going off on almost every Screen. Bright red lights burnt purple and blue images in my eyes. It was like I was looking at the sun everywhere I turned. And the sound. The high-pitched wail of the sirens made my ears ring.

My eyes darted around the empty bar. I was still sitting in the exact same spot where I'd fallen asleep. I didn't have long to look outside, but I saw people running to look up at the Screens amidst the strong wind whipping posters of election campaigns and wanted signs around every which way. I quickly focused my attention back on the Screen at the bar, just like the people running outside in the streets, suddenly all standing still, mouths agape as the Screens lit up.

It was worse than anything I could've imagined. Cincinnati was an inferno, a burning abyss. I thought back to an image I'd seen on the Screen in grade school the day we talked about "religion." Though I didn't know where it came from or when it was completed, one stood out: *The Last Judgement* by Jan van Eyck. It was like the image in my mind had become reality.

I heard their shrill screams as I watched the cameraman recording people pounding on doors, trying to find shelter. Trying to get help. There was dust everywhere, making it hard to see what was going on, although anyone watching knew.

There was fire everywhere. The main electric lines in Cincinnati had collapsed, splintered and broken. I clutched my stomach. I could see what looked like bodies crushed under some of the power lines, but I didn't want to believe it. I felt like I was going to be sick.

Temperatures neared 1,200°F, per the news report, but who knew how accurate that was. The more I watched, the more I believed that was lower than reality. Fire had taken one of the main telecommunications buildings in the heart of the city, and the power lines leading to and from the structure carried the fire's rage further from the heart to the outskirts. But more horrifying than the vicious flames, the screaming people, those running and driving like mad, the helicopters blowing the thick dust into tornado-like runs along the ground, and the sirens burning holes in my eardrums, was the fault line.

What originally looked like a small fissure from an aggravated earthquake had expanded substantially and ran from the city center through the building consumed by fire, which I finally made out to have gotten that way from being split down the middle, one half collapsing into the crack. From there, the fault ran all the way through the city to the suburbs, only miles from the nearest border along that side of the Dome. The fault was immense, and views of the streets surrounding the area showed the pavement broken and crumbling downward, taking everything with it. Parts of the road even jutted vertically, creating mountainous forms in the city streets. The crevasse was hundreds of feet wide from what I could see from the aerial drone footage of the city. A list of the rising death toll ran below it, and playbacks of emergency calls were interspersed between reporters trying, and failing, to describe what was going on.

The drone moved closer and closer to the fault until you could see inside. It was all black, but deep down, who knew how far, bright red and orange liquid glowed like embers. Lava. Was it possible it went down that far?

"Adam!" I heard my name being yelled through the glass door along with a loud pounding. Startled, I jumped out of my chair and had to catch myself from falling. I grabbed my chest instinctively as I raced to the door, yanking it open. It was Linda. Her red hair was wild in the wind, and the wrinkles on her face seemed deeper and more concentrated than ever. She looked scared, and I couldn't blame her. She grew up in Cincinnati and had family there . . . if they were still alive.

"Adam!" she yelled again in relief and pulled me into a tight hug. "I've been trying to call your apartment! Even called the landlord and had my ass chewed out when I showed up out of the blue. You need to get out of the city! To the Border!"

What was she talking about? I never heard her mention the Border, the area connecting the Dome to the outside world; the Las Vegas station lay right on it. Now she was talking about getting out. That didn't make an ounce of sense in my mind. Why leave the city?

"Adam!" She snapped her fingers in front of my face, and her scream drew the attention of those standing near the entrance to the bar. The door hinge was broken and didn't close properly without forcefully shoving it. Everyone outside could hear what we said. It wasn't safe to draw attention to yourself, or trust people in general, especially not those with Monitors. The Heads of State saw everything they needed through them. I swore that was how they knew things they weren't supposed to. At least, that was my mother's conspiracy theory. Must have been true or else how would anyone have known to drop by after she shot herself?

"Adam, are you listening to me?" Linda yelled, and I had to grab her hand to stop her from smacking me. I even laughed at her out of confusion and shock from what I'd just seen.

"What?" I asked, but the laughing seemed all wrong. It all seemed wrong. "Why are you yelling? You're acting insane!" I paused, thinking. I wasn't sure exactly what to do or say. I was confused, and my thoughts were clouded for once with something other than the constant buzzing, though I wasn't enjoying the screaming and blaring sirens pouring from the Screens that replaced it.

"The Border." She gasped, out of breath. "I . . . I need someone to get me there. I have to get to the station and to Cincinnati. I have to get to m-my family . . ." She looked back over her shoulder at one of the Screens that was brightly lit, even with the glare of the rising sun.

"You don't need me," I said. I needed a way to get back there myself, but what was the chance of seeing the girl when the station was probably loaded with people coming in from Cincinnati and others going there to get people out? The chance was slim to begin with. "They're probably going to be shutting down the stations soon anyway," I said, trying to find an excuse to stay. Every part of me told me to stay away from the stations. That was where most people were going to go, and crowded did not equal safe. If the catastrophe was truly as bad as the media was portraying, it was reasonable to say the Trams would be closing soon. The government needed to control whatever was going on. And what the fuck was going on? It was a nightmare, but we'd seen worse since the times of the War, hadn't we? Then again, that hadn't been for decades. Still, we should be prepared for disaster. Right?

"I can't go alone," Linda whined at last, seeming slightly younger as she stood before me with tears beginning to well in her eyes: my laid-back, sarcastic manager replaced with a frightened child. I'd never seen this side of her before. "Please, Adam. You're the only one I know who goes there so frequently. I can't even remember what stops to get off at. You know I never use the Trams."

That I did know, but she had a Monitor. She could easily use it to find her way to the Border; it was an internal GPS. Yet, it couldn't erase her primal fear of the unfamiliar. I knew she rarely obeyed the automatic commands "suggesting" visits to the stations; the suggestions, among millions of others, existing solely for the profit of the Regime and any corporations willing to pay the price for the data trends stored within the implant. I guess her Monitor hadn't eaten away her brain quite yet.

She was scared of being alone with what was happening. There was also the fact that Linda's husband had died at the Border, just like that woman I'd seen two days earlier. It was painful for her to go anywhere near there.

"Okay," I finally said after a minute, trying to sound calm. "Anything for you." It was a way there, I told myself, but it seemed all wrong. I was finally getting the chance to go back, but I didn't want to. I didn't want to bring myself any closer to the infernal mess and that crack into nothingness.

In the end, Linda's persistent pleading dragged me from the bar. More than that, I wanted to find the girl. It was a shred of hope that I stupidly clung to, but I didn't have anything to lose. Unlike Linda, I didn't have any family, and I was pretty sure the neighbor's cat that visited my apartment every so often to catch mice wasn't exactly fond of me. I was alone and had been for a very long time.

CHAPTER 7

"I'm sorry, boy, no more passengers," a security agent who spoke and moved more like a machine than a human said as I stood in a line of hundreds of people at the station. I didn't see his eyes through his black helmet, but I knew he was looking at my history. "Been to the station a few times in the past couple weeks." There was a hint of suspicion in his voice. "Odd for a man of your class."

"I keep getting orders to come here, sir." My Monitor wasn't discernable from the buzzing of the hundreds of others at the tracks. The agent wouldn't know that I didn't have one and that nothing told me to visit the Border Station besides myself.

"Please." Linda pushed a man standing close behind me out of the way and stood next to me at the control desk. She held her hands up in a pleading way to the security agent. "My family is in Cincinnati." She pointed at me. "He's trying to help me get there to save them. Please, have a heart."

I stood out in any social crowd, so I was used to saying and doing all the wrong things, but that didn't mean that I didn't know what was right and what was wrong to do. What Linda said to the agent was wrong. We were taught to never let our emotions get the best of us, ever, especially in front of someone who had the power to kill us with the touch of a button—the preferred weapon of those in power. With one move, the agent could press it and send a signal to the Database to have her Monitor destroyed. When that happened, the whole brain went with it. Swift justice, or injustice, with no consequences for the executioner.

I grabbed Linda's arm to pull her away from the desk as the security agent raised his hand to slap her in the face. How dare she have spoken out of turn. "I'm so sorry, sir. She has been suffering from mental illness for years," I lied quickly and yanked on Linda's arm as she began to protest.

"Sounds like the two of you need your levels fixed. The Monitors should be taking care of that," the agent spat with a scowl I knew was there under that helmet.

"Come on, Linda, let's get out of here. We'll find another—"

Linda cut me off as she ripped her arm from my grip and shoved the agent from across the counter with one quick thrust of her arms. "You son of a bitch! I'll be damned if you stand in the way of me and my family! I will report you to—"

I jerked backward as blood splattered across my face, and Linda slumped sideways into my arms. My whole body shook as I looked down at her. A gaping hole gushed blood from the back of her head. My eyes widened, and I risked a glance up at the agent. His gloved hand was on a small black box with an indiscernible button attached to his black leather belt.

"She should have known better. I hope you will from now on."

I staggered back, my legs shaking, and let Linda's body fall to the ground without meaning to. There was already another agent walking my way to collect her. I wanted to scream and tell them to leave her alone, but I didn't. She had a family. She had a business. Then she had nothing at all. Like my mother, like the old woman at the tracks two days ago. Of all the horrors I'd seen, nothing could've prepared me for this moment.

A couple of people behind me stared at Linda's body with wide eyes, and a baby cried as its father patted its back and tried to soothe it. Other people just stared at their feet. Others looked like nothing had happened at all.

My hands shook at my sides as the other security agents posted around the station entrance came over to help remove Linda's body. I needed to get out of here immediately. They were going to find out I didn't have a Monitor. Most likely, they were going to kill me for lying. It was bad, very bad.

I had just witnessed a murder. Cincinnati was in flames. Things were going to change, and quickly. I'd been wrong when I thought we'd overcome this disaster.

Red sirens wailed and spun in circles around the Tram station, sending beams of crimson light around the building. The Screens projected images of Untouchables in the outskirts of Cincinnati dead in large groups from the raging fire. People in suits held up recording devices as the other half of the telecommunications building that had been split in half began to fall, sending debris and dust over people below. And here I was inside the station with a woman's blood on my face and clothes.

The agent behind the control counter wiped a spot of it from his helmet but let the other splatters remain on the counter. Linda would serve as a warning for everyone in the station. She should've listened to what she was told and never, ever have acted against those above her.

My head was spinning, and it felt like there was a heavy weight pressing down on my chest. If I stayed here, I'd do something I'd regret and end up dead. I knew this was true, so I turned around and started walking out of the building, away from Linda and the security agents that had finally made it to her corpse. Then I ran.

I sucked in deep breaths and clutched at my sides as my feet hit the hot pavement. It was mid-afternoon, and the Screens reflected sunbeams on billboards and the sides of buildings. Ads still poured out of the monolithic devices, but most showed images of devastation and live footage from Cincinnati in place of some popular rapper's new album and a designer's latest collection. Sirens continued to blare throughout the city and its outskirts. I saw Untouchables huddled in side alleys, and except for the people making their way toward the station, there were barely any people or machines to be seen in the typically crowded streets of downtown Vegas. Usually, the sounds of horns honking and pedestrians yelling were heard around the clock, but that was no longer the case. People weren't even watching the Screens outside.

"Shit!" I screamed louder than I meant to as I ran straight into a small Hispanic woman walking with her son toward the station.

"Watch where you're going!" she yelled as she pulled her son closer to her and hurried down the road. For an instant, I wondered what she might've said at a time when we all spoke different languages.

"Wait!" I called after her before I could stop myself. She was probably going to report me for causing a disturbance and might accuse me of trying to harm her or her son. I couldn't blame her for being frightened of me: a tall, skinny white guy with wild blonde hair and blood smeared across his face and shirt. I didn't want to be around when an Officer showed up to investigate, but I had to risk it. "Excuse me, ma'am!" I called again as I caught up with her and her son. The little boy buried his face in his mother's skirt.

"I'm sorry," I said hurriedly. "I didn't mean to run into you like that."

"Please, leave us alone," she said, breathless.

"I don't want to hurt you," I assured her. "I just wanted to say I was sorry."

"What are you even doing out here?" she asked with her eyebrows creased together. "Didn't you get the signal to stay home? That's where I'm going and where you should be. It isn't safe. Your Monitor should've told you." While she spoke, she looked at her son and anywhere else but me. I imagined what she was thinking: Do not look at the blood. He will go away. Don't look at the blood. He's just a kid . . . Please, don't hurt my son.

I looked at her, pretending to be confused, then rubbed the

back of my head as if I had the implant. "I don't know why I didn't get the signal."

"Maybe it's jammed," she said and picked up her son. "You look lost, though." I wanted to tell her that I felt lost. I envied the little boy and how she protected him in her arms.

She glanced at me for a moment, her eyes flitting to the spots of blood on my cheek, then pushed past and kept walking quickly toward the station, her eyes glued to the sidewalk.

"They won't let you go anywhere," I called after her, but she didn't turn around.

The Monitors were ordering people to stay home or go to the stations in order to get there. Maybe the government didn't want to cause a panic. I felt like the only one who was actually panicking. Someone was just murdered at the station! Someone I knew, but the woman didn't know that. I wondered if it would've made her turn around.

I ducked into a side alley as I heard the siren of an Officer down the road. It was barely audible over the emergency sirens coming from the Screens. I quickly crouched behind a dumpster, though I could still see the street clearly from my view, and wiped the blood from my face with the sleeve of my shirt.

"Breathe, Adam. Just breathe," I whispered to myself as I looked out of the alley and saw the Officer's black autonome blow past. When it was gone, the figure I saw was much more alarming.

It was her. The girl.

She was standing on the sidewalk on the other side of the street, staring at the dumpster. I held my breath and waited. She stood there for a moment, then turned and headed in the direction of the station.

No! I thought. I had to warn her, which meant leaving safety behind.

I ran out of the alley without another thought and didn't even look before crossing the street over to her. "Wait!" I yelled. "Wait, you can't go there!"

She stopped walking and turned around to face me. I froze

dead in my tracks.

"Do you honestly think I'm going to the station to try and catch a Tram?" She rolled her eyes. "Do I look like an idiot to you? There's no way they're letting anyone out of the city now. I know what they're doing. All the lower classes are there. If anything goes wrong, they'll be the first to go. Wouldn't that be convenient? The elite are already out of Cincinnati, safe and sound, and they're evacuating the other cities just in case." She took a deep breath and continued, "We're going to the station because we have to get through the Border. It's the closest access point nearby. We have to get through it. We have to find a way to Cincinnati, Adam."

After everything she said, all I could respond was, "How do you know my name?"

"A perk of having a Monitor, but you wouldn't know about that, would you?"

I forced my gaping mouth shut. "How did—"

"It doesn't matter, and I'm not here to sell you out to the agents, okay? We need to go. We have to get out of here."

"I'm not going anywhere with you," I said quickly, not entirely convinced of what I was saying, but fear had taken over once more. I had intended to search this girl out, but she knew something about me that would kill me if she let it slip. What else did she know?

She grabbed my hand and started pulling me toward the station. "If we stand around, we make ourselves targets." I tried to shake her off, but I didn't want to hurt her.

"An agent just murdered my boss in there," I replied. "They aren't going to like it when I show back up."

She turned around for a second to look me in the eyes. "I'm so sorry . . ." She looked genuinely sad, but it didn't stop her. She continued pulling me along toward the station, determined. "They won't see you, Adam. Not with the hordes of people."

"Stop saying my name! You don't know who I am!" I spat angrily without meaning to. Someone had just been killed there! What didn't she understand?

"My name is Eve Wesson," she said simply. "Nice to meet you too."

Eve's free hand tightly gripped the small bag she'd dropped when I ran into her the other day, though I guessed that her grip on me was even stronger. I didn't want to admit that a small part of me was excited about walking back to the station with the revealed intention of breaking through the Border, but there it was, trying to fight the fear and anxiety threatening to overwhelm me. Who was this mysterious girl who knew I wasn't like everyone else, and why did she want my help? I was torn. It was dumb to blindly follow a stranger, but she seemed to really care about the people at the station who could all die as easily as Linda. She seemed to want to help them, but what good was escaping?

"What's in the bag?" I asked as I picked up the pace in time with her, giving in to curiosity.

"Bombs." She said it as if she were talking about something as innocent as candy.

"What? You'll never get that past security, even on the exterior." Security agents were posted not just inside but all around the Border Station.

"I did two days ago," she replied casually and looked back at me with a small smile.

I remembered kneeling to pick up the small bag off the ground after I'd run into her two days earlier. It seemed like a lifetime ago at this point. How had she managed to get in with bombs? Security systems were in place to prevent that, supposedly.

"Actually," she began, "they're Monitors, and a bunch of them. They weren't cheap, but I've been collecting them for years now." She paused to think, then added with a slight laugh, "I wonder if yours is buried in there somewhere." Seeing the confusion written in the deep lines on my forehead, she continued, "I'm a thief, you could say. I'm not proud of it, but I had to do something to stay alive."

Conflicting emotions surged again inside me, but I had no

time to ask her for a deeper explanation. We were standing across the street from the station, its concrete façade appearing more like a prison than a stop along the myriad Tram routes across the Regime. I wanted to run from what was surely death waiting for us, but I was equally intrigued and wanted to see the girl pull off an escape that not many people had accomplished and lived to see another day. I was skeptical and knew I could run from her right now, but something inside me begged to stay.

"Great, so you have a bunch of Monitors stashed in that bag of yours. How are you going to do anything with them?" She had to give me something if she wanted my help.

"At the Border the other day, when we ran into one another," she started, "I was there to pick up one of these." She pulled a small black control panel from her pocket, just like the one the security agent had used to murder Linda. My fists clenched into tight balls at the thought. I knew now that I had to help Eve. The plan was a mystery, but if there was even the slightest chance that we could help save people, I had to do it. For Linda, for my mother, for the boy in his mother's arms, and for everyone else who didn't stand a chance.

There was a telephone booth at the corner of the street on which we stood. Once, they were used by visitors of the country, but they'd become useless decorations. They still worked, however, as long as someone paid. People generally used them as private locations to get high or have sex, so I was alarmed when Eve pulled me into the booth at the corner of the walkway. My heart pounded in my chest as she closed the door and we were no longer visible from the outside, not that there was anyone to see us but the Screens and the Monitors.

The Monitors. She still had one.

"You're lying! I know you are!" I screamed. Monitors regulated emotions and delinquent behavioral traits. If she'd really been planning an escape through the Dome—a criminal violation punishable by death—her Monitor should've autocorrected her thoughts and redirected them into something more "positive."

"Your Monitor would know what you've been thinking! It would stop you and—"

Eve reached up and pulled the earpiece that was attached to the Monitor from her ear. The pieces were typically connected to the device inserted in the back of the head and allowed people to hear the audio that sometimes went with the images and neural commands. Most people had the earpieces surgically implanted along with the Monitor like the old woman did. Either way, Eve couldn't have pulled it out if it was real. That was the price of the Monitor. We weren't allowed to take it out. But it was for our own good; we were never allowed to forget.

"It's not real, so you can calm down," she said evenly. "I reconfigured it. All it can do is receive media signals."

She kept amazing me. "I thought you said—"

"I don't have one. I'm like you."

"Then how did you know who I was?"

"I've been watching you for a while now. It's scary what you can learn about a person just from observing them."

I went to say something else, but she put her hand to my mouth to stop me. Her face glowed in the low light of the space, and I vaguely noticed a syringe with a rusted needle lying empty on the grime-covered floor of the booth.

"We don't have a lot of time, so you have to listen to me carefully." Her breath was hot against my face. "There's already a weak point in the Border. A trip in the electric system. We're going to throw a couple of these Monitors at the tracks underneath it, and I'm going to push this button. The explosion of the devices should cause a short in the electric wall. That's our way out. It should disappear long enough for us to get through. We're going to have to be fast because—"

"I thought there was already a short in the wall." I noticed the past few times a maintenance warning along a section of the station wall that separated the outside of the Dome from the inside of the Regime. Behind the maintenance barrier, there looked like there was already a hole in the synthesized wall. It had a pair of tracks running underneath it that were currently shut down because of the maintenance, though there was no one there working on it.

"They want you to think there's a short, but it's just a way to test people. I was watching it the other day, and I saw a stray dog try to go through it . . ." She grimaced. "The minute you step onto the tracks, thinking it's a passage through the barrier, you end up like that woman who disappeared under the Tram. You're dead."

So it was a way to weed out discontents. It made sense, yet it still made me unbearably angry. What a convenient way to get rid of undesirables and Untouchables who decided they wanted to get the fuck out of this miserable place. Those that thought they had a chance. I felt the overwhelming urge to bury my face in my hands and cry. I wanted to cry for Linda, for the old woman, for my mother, and for everyone else who was so easily forgotten by the system.

"I want to make them pay too," Eve said softly and squeezed my hand. "The ones who let people die and don't stop to care for one second. We have to focus on getting to Cincinnati, though. The fault is getting bigger, and the fire is spreading through the surrounding cities. This isn't killing the people we hate; it's killing the people who can't do anything to save themselves."

My determination gave way to doubt. "We are those people," I said and looked her in the eyes. "What can we do? We're nobodies. At least I know I am."

Eve frowned. "I have to believe that isn't true." She shoved the bag into my hands as she finished. "I know you can do this, bartender."

So, she had been watching me.

CHAPTER 8

"Don't hold your breath. I can't have you passing out on me, and I need your help to make this work," Eve whispered as we walked hand in hand through the entrance of the station. She insisted it was crucial that we stay together, and when she'd taken my hand, I hadn't resisted. I had nothing to lose. I just hoped she couldn't feel me shaking from the nerves.

The initial security system didn't send any distress signals to the agents who barely took any notice of us as we walked in. I assumed I was on some watch list at this point, but then again, why would anyone care about some frightened guy who ran out of the station after his boss was killed by one of their agents?

"I promise to breathe," I whispered back. Our feet made a soft tapping sound as we walked between the hordes of people standing in line to get tickets we knew they were never going to get, and those waiting around staring at the images dancing in their heads that no one saw but them. Some people talked with one another about useless things they'd seen on the Screens, but they were few and far between. If anyone stopped to take notice of us, we might seem strange to them. Heterosexual couples were in the minority. Sure, some men were with women, but it wasn't as popular. I only had one hetero friend: Mike. He only had one, too, that one being me. Still, it wasn't frowned upon, just slightly strange since anyone could be with whomever they wanted, or be whomever they wanted, for that matter.

"How are we going to get through the scanners without passes?" I asked after a minute.

Right as I asked, Eve tapped her forearm, where an invisible chip housed all personal information about her, in addition to her bank account and credit card information, if she possessed them. "It's already there. You have one too."

A surprised look came over my face.

"Don't ask," she quickly said when I started to do just that. "I'll explain later. They're passes to Houston, which will work to get us through the main building and onto the platform where the wall is. That's all we need." I didn't ask, but theories raced through my head. There was no way to have ticket information stored in the circuits of the identification chip without personally requesting it. The information was linked to my bank account, but I never made the purchase. Therefore, someone would need to have hacked into the system for the pass to be there. I glanced at Eve. Who was she? How did she have that ability? I pushed the questions away and focused on not screwing up.

The station was enormous and separated into several different sections, including the main concrete building housing the central identification checkpoint and ticketing areas. The adjacent buildings that were partly exposed to the outside through openings at the back offered the closest view of the Dome you could get anywhere in the city, as well as a way for hundreds of Trams to exit on their destinations around the Regime. Some Tram routes didn't need to go outside the Dome to reach their destinations, but for a lot of them, it was quicker that way, and if anyone who wanted to get away from the Regime managed to open a Tram door while en route, hoping to escape, invisible lasers in between the doors would kill them before they had the chance to try. Attempting to leave the Dome was generally considered a death sentence, and here we were, trying to do just that.

Agents stood at every corner and checkpoint in and

between the buildings. The ones that weren't dealing with the angry people trying to get through to Cincinnati—and those trying to convince themselves there was anywhere safe to go— stood like motionless statues, their black helmets reflecting the bright fluorescent lights of the Screens. The bright orange and red flames from the drone footage at the heart of the devastation flickered across one man's helmet. I wondered if he was the one who killed Linda, but it was impossible to tell. They all looked exactly the same, and there was no sign of blood on any of them. The only indication that she'd been killed at all were the blood splatters still at the desk of the main ID checkpoint where I'd stood next to her. I'd felt my knees buckle when I saw it, half expecting to find her still lying there. But her body was long gone, and I didn't recognize any of the people who'd been standing around me when it'd happened. It would be impossible, though, in the hordes of people. I'd never seen the station this crowded, and it was barely possible to move on normal days.

Those who'd bought tickets before the disaster escalated were allowed to pass through the main building and out into the various levels that made up the departure and arrival zones where the Trams waited, hovering inches above the pulsing blue lights of the electric tracks beneath.

We easily made it through the scanners and found ourselves on the first level of the departure zone where the Trams and the invisible barrier of the Dome leveled with the ground. It was the same area outside the central ticket and control building where we'd unofficially met two days ago. Again, the image of the woman bleeding and burning on the tracks formed in my mind, and I had to shake my head to make it go away. I forced myself to look around the room to take my mind off it. Instead of people rushing north and south, in and out of the building, people were just standing around everywhere. None of the Trams were boarding yet, so everyone was stuck in limbo, forced to watch the images on their Monitors or those on the big, bright, blaring Screens.

"Delayed – Boarding TBD" scrolled across the long, sleek

metal frames of the Trams in bright orange letters. All the windows were currently tinted so that the announcement was the only thing visible. It amazed me how many Trams there were; their massive bodies lined up in rows pointed toward the Dome. They were so streamlined that you couldn't tell where the doors were until they opened or where one car ended and the other began.

Above the stalled Trams, red, flashing sirens were posted in vertical lines down the ceiling that sheltered the tracks. The sun was just dipping below the line of the roof, making it even harder to see against the gleaming Trams and blinding Screens.

I watched as a cloud passed over, making it easier to see the Dome. It was nearly invisible, but the reflections of the Screens covering the walls of the station's desolate concrete interior and exterior gave it away. They were faint but still clear to anyone looking close enough. I seemed to be the only one watching the artificial lights bounce off the synthesized barrier between us and the wasteland beyond the Border. The wasteland we'd soon be in if Eve's plan worked.

I looked around again at the people all crowded together with barely enough room to breathe between them. Most had dazed looks on their faces, their eyes glossed over as images danced in their heads. For those who had real Monitors, the implants were always turned on, and the user could simply tune into the broadcasts, shows, Internet, and anything else they had open and running, or they could try to ignore the constant distraction, like the way I tried to ignore the images on the Screens that never ceased. You could usually tell when a person was paying attention to their Monitor, though, because they got a faraway look in their eyes. Sometimes they raised an eyebrow or opened their mouths ever so slightly, reacting with minimal emotion, and I wondered if the ones doing that now were watching the broadcasts from Cincinnati or something completely unrelated. Something completely irrelevant.

The Screens around us showed news of the fires and the

dead alongside mind-numbing reality shows about people too self-consumed to care about those losing their lives halfway across the Regime. That was in addition to the sirens still blaring and the red warning lights reflecting off the steel beams supporting the exterior section of the station. It hurt my eyes to look at it all, and the sounds were deafening. Even outside the main building, the agitated conversations at the ticket areas and checkpoints of those trying to get through echoed. Inside, there weren't any windows. Just the dark concrete walls and blinding fluorescent tubes illuminating the high ceilings. Absolutely nothing to distract from the Screens. At least out here I could see the Dome. But it wasn't enough. I was willing to risk my life for something different. Something better. Something silent.

I scanned the invisible wall that surrounded the area and only dissipated when the Trams passed outside the Dome and it dematerialized for a fraction of a second. The blue-white light of the electricity was barely detectable, but I could see the sparking section: the break in the wall that I'd noticed the other day. I looked at Eve, and she nodded her head ever so slightly. My fingers, weaved between hers, tightened around her hand, and we started to walk toward the break that was, conveniently so, next to the track with the Tram destined for Houston. "You're brilliant," I said to Eve.

"Thank you." She smiled widely.

I'd already taken some of the Monitors out of her bag and was messing with them nervously in my pocket.

Just breathe, Adam. Just breathe.

We were standing before the Tram to Houston far too soon. "Boarding in 30 minutes" flashed in white electric letters across its sleek metal exterior. If her plan went wrong, and I knew it could, I expected to die and never get to know the mysterious girl I should've left the minute she told me she was watching me. But I hadn't. I wanted more than anything to know her. My life was unimportant. She made me hope that I could do more than be a bartender and live in squalor for the rest of my life. She made me believe that I might not be useless, that someone might care if I was gone. But maybe I was just fooling myself.

Eve let go of my hand and did something that surprised me more than everything else she'd done up to this point. She took my face in her small hands and pushed up on her toes to kiss me. Instantly, fireworks exploded in my stomach, and every part of me fell victim to her touch. I'd never felt that intensely in my entire life. She pulled away from me after a moment, and I immediately wanted her back. It felt like I needed her to breathe.

"I'm sorry. I just . . ." She stared at me like she had the day at the station when I first saw her, like she was waiting for something, and just like I had that day, I didn't know what to do. She seemed to deflate. "I'm sorry," she said again, looking slightly embarrassed. "If we make it out of here, I promise I'll try to explain everything."

Clearly, there was a lot I didn't understand. I went to ask her what she meant, but she cut me off. "Now" was all she said as she started to walk around to the opposite side of the Tram where the break was.

My stomach knotted. It was happening. There wasn't any more time to think.

I started to sweat, and my hands shook. What was I doing? Chaos was going to erupt once the Monitors exploded and the wall lapsed. I didn't want anyone in the station to be blamed and become the distraction we needed to escape, but this was going to do more harm than good, wasn't it? I didn't even know what Eve's plan was, though.

I looked at the people standing around us. I told myself we'd make it up to them, eventually. I desperately hoped we would. That was if it worked and we made it out alive ourselves.

Fear gnawed at my insides. Nothing made sense anymore, but I couldn't give in to it. I had to do something to try to help people like Linda. I couldn't just wait around hoping things would get better. It was time to act.

Now, Adam. Now!

I sucked in a deep breath as I rounded the corner to the break and knelt like I was tying my shoe. With a last look over my shoulder to make sure there weren't any agents looking our way, I tossed three of the Monitors at the break. They slid and made it just under the invisible wall to rest in the divide between it and the tracks leading beyond the Regime's border. I hung in suspense as I stared at the small computers destined once for people's brains, their silver components and wires connecting to the earpieces glinting in the afternoon light and reflecting the blue glow of the electric tracks.

I glanced up at Eve, who was standing a few feet away from me, as she pushed the button on the small black device in her pocket. Just like the one the agent had used to signal the Monitor database and end Linda's life in a fraction of a second, the device in Eve's palm caused the three Monitors to explode in an array of white, blue, and orange sparks that erupted with a loud hiss into the air.

"What's going on?" a security agent yelled from the corner of the tracks nearest to us as soon as it happened. The sirens blared loudly, and the Screens drummed incessantly on; plenty of people took no notice of the blast against this noise, but those standing next to the Houston Tram gasped, and a woman even yelled. I was surprised it warranted any reaction at all.

But I was wrong. My mouth hung open in shock, and suddenly, everything erupted into chaos. A man behind the woman who screamed shoved her to the ground and ran toward the now apparent break in the wall. Sparks were raining down, but it wasn't anything that could kill a person. The wall was dead where the Monitors had exploded, the barrier between the Regime and the outside world broken; it was appearing to fail all around the exterior of the station. Blue, white, and orange danced in vein-like patterns along the once invisible surface, revealing the electrical makeup of the barrier. More people began to yell, and then they were running everywhere. I stood up quickly to see several agents take out Tasers and other weapons and begin to assault people. "Calm down!" I heard one yell, though he looked to be inflicting the most harm.

"Adam, come on!" Eve screamed. "Adam!"

She was standing on the opposite side of the failing wall near the glowing blue tracks leading off into the distant desert. She was waving me down, and I could barely see her through the rush of people exiting. It was mass hysteria. Did they run because they wanted to be free, or because they didn't know, for once in their lives, what to do? Whatever the cause, I hoped they made it to wherever they needed to go before the Officers showed up. That was when it would get really bad.

I'd started running toward Eve when an agent hit me on the back with a baton and my body was sent flying to the ground. I flipped myself over as his weapon came down again, hitting the concrete ground instead this time. I couldn't see his face, but I recognized his voice: the agent that killed Linda.

"I should've known it was you! You should've been the one to die, not the hag!" Just like that, he seemed to get an idea. He pressed the button on the small black device on his belt hard, but nothing happened. He pressed it again, still nothing.

He'd expected it to work the way it had on Linda and who knew how many others. Usually, when the agents pressed the button, it latched onto the wireless signal of the person's Monitor it was directed at, confirming a connection. When the system was first being developed, an agent had killed a hundred people at once trying to get one man. That was before the technology was put in place to target specific signals.

Once the confirmation went through—a way to tell that the person did indeed have a Monitor—then the automated request was sent to the database for it to be destroyed. The process typically took all of a couple seconds.

Not for me.

"You!" he screamed furiously as he realized I didn't have a Monitor. "You fucking dissident!" He lifted his weapon once more to strike, but I had enough time while he was trying to kill me with the touch of a button to get to my feet. I jumped to the side and avoided his swing, then turned on my heel as I saw him grab for his gun. I heard the shot go off and heard more screams but didn't turn around to see what, or who, he hit. Guilt came over me like a tsunami, but all I could see was Eve. She'd turned and started running. I followed as fast as I could.

We were outside the reach of the Regime, in theory. All that was around us were deserted buildings, dead plants, and dirt. There were people everywhere, screaming, the sirens of the Officers screeched behind us, and shots continued to go off inside the station. We'd created our own personal Cincinnati, Eve and I. We turned a "quiet" evening into a nightmare for everyone there, but I had to trust she knew what she was doing. She told me she was a thief, a criminal, but I desperately wanted to believe her intentions were good, despite what I heard and saw all around me.

I finally caught up to her, and she risked a glance at me. "Thank you!" She looked like she wanted to say a million different things, but we weren't safe. Not yet.

Sometimes we do things to save other people, even though they may be bad. I had no idea what Eve had gone through to end up in her situation. My own mother killed herself to protect me.

Every child was implanted with a Monitor, but that didn't mean every child grew up with one. My mother hired someone to remove mine; it was a gruesome, bloody mess that nearly killed both of us, but it worked. A week after it happened, the doctor who performed the surgery was tracked down by the State and killed for his crime. He'd once been respected, performing countless implant surgeries, and then he was forgotten. That meant the only person left who knew about the surgery was my mother. I was too young to know what had happened, so I wasn't a risk, but she was, and the people who found the doctor knew about her involvement in the situation.

The Regime kept a record of every birth. Everyone was

supposed to have a Monitor, and the government generally knew about those that didn't. Unfortunately, it was still illegal to directly question individuals about their associations with Monitors due to privacy laws, ironically. My mother knew that if she took herself out of the equation and hid me, I wouldn't, in theory, be found. For all the Regime knew, Adam Locke was dead, and Adam Krichmar had nothing to do with him, thanks to my mother.

She told me where to go, and when I saw her kill herself, I ran as far away from her as I could. I didn't understand it, and I was scared. She told me if I told anyone about her, I'd die too. So, I kept my mouth shut and grew up with other kids in a foster home pretending I wasn't different, pretending my earpiece was real. I met other people who were like me, though I never told them, and they were all eventually found. The Regime had surgeries performed on them, but most of the kids who didn't have Monitors were older, and it was harder to perform the implantation on them. It usually resulted in their deaths. Still, there were other people out there who lacked the system. Usually, they were the children of Untouchables whose parents had given birth under the radar. The Regime didn't bother with their population because it typically took care of itself, thanks to contaminated water and inadequate food supplies. I wondered if Eve came from a family of them.

After we made it through the break in the Dome wall, we ran for miles until we found a ravine far enough away from where most people exiting the Border went. You couldn't see us from where the others were, but we couldn't see them either. We had to find a better place.

I kept waiting for Eve to clue me in on her big plan to get to Cincinnati. Eventually, I fell asleep instead.

I dreamt about the countryside. That, for one, wasn't out of the ordinary. Many of us did. We dreamt of taking time away from the daily drudge of existence to enjoy life. I don't think any of us truly knew how to do that anymore, and how could we? That was something reserved for those of us who didn't have to work away most of our lives to barely make enough to support ourselves, let alone our families. I was lucky I had only myself. Or, at least, that was what I kept telling myself.

I'd dreamt this before. I was in a grassy field sometime at the beginning of summer. I could hear the songs of various birds, but I had no idea what kind they were. I hardly took notice of them in the city because they couldn't be heard over the blare of mechanic horns, the music, the electric buzz of the Monitors, and the clatter of feet on streets carrying empty souls to their empty jobs where they were made to feel that they were making enough money to live. That was one of the many, many lies of our society.

In the dream, in the field, I couldn't hear that noise. There was sound, but it was different. It was peaceful. There was the purr of a cat lying in the sun next to me, its legs stretched out in front of it as I stroked its fur. I watched as its tail flicked rhythmically and its paws moved with the flex of its claws, and I wished I had internal weapons like the creature. The only one I possessed was my brain, unattended by a Monitor. What good was that to anyone but myself? I wasn't serving any larger purpose. But the alternate route to my own was the one my mother had taken. Something about the breeze that blew softly over my skin and the purring cat in my dream told me that wasn't the right choice.

I looked up with a smile on my face, the songbirds still chattering away in distant trees. Not far off, I could make out a girl standing under a tall willow, like one I'd once heard about in a feature on extinct species.

Her smooth, dark brown hair was loose and flowed in the wind like the leaves of the tree. She was beautiful, wearing a thin dress through which her olive skin could be seen. I wanted to touch her and feel her warmth under my palms, but when I tried to move, I was stuck to the ground. My legs wouldn't budge, and my arms couldn't bend. I was utterly frozen.

She stared at me fixedly, and while she did, the world around us changed. The grass turned brown around my body;

the cat stood, hissed with a raised back, then ran off; the wind became hot; and birds started to fall from the sky, dead. Dust blew around, blurring my view of her. She opened her mouth, maybe to call for me, maybe to scream, but she never moved.

A crack formed in the middle of the ground. It was a hairline fracture at first, then quickly grew until it was hundreds of feet wide, just like the one in Cincinnati. It ran diagonally across the ground, separating us. It never reached me but grew closer and closer to her until she was standing at the edge, the black and red lava creeping toward her. I tried to close my eyes so I didn't have to watch her die, but they did not obey. Then she was gone, just like that. A dream turned into a nightmare.

I woke up thrashing around and screaming.

"Adam! Adam, shhh," Eve said as she grabbed my arms to stop me from shaking. "Are you okay?"

I sat up in an instant and looked around. We were still the only two in the ravine. I hoped my scream hadn't alerted anyone nearby to our presence. "I . . . it was a bad dream," I said, still stunned.

Only then did I realize the girl in the dream was Eve. Her olive skin and dark brown hair were exactly the same. There was no mistaking it.

"Are you sure? You kept saying my name . . ." Eve trailed off. "I didn't know if I should wake you."

My heart started to pound. I'd had that same dream before; the only thing that was different was the fault. I pictured the crack in Cincinnati when I'd first seen it on the Screens, and how it'd seemed endless, darkness stretching so far down into the Earth that you could see the glow of lava. It haunted me when I was awake, so it didn't shock me that it appeared in my dream. But it wasn't just any dream. I'd dreamt of that field before, and in those same dreams, I'd seen the girl. But she wasn't just any girl. It was *her*. Eve. That meant I'd dreamt of her long before I'd seen her at the station.

"I called your name?" I asked, trying to sound like I had

no idea what she was talking about, but she raised an eyebrow. She knew I was lying.

"I dreamt you died." I only gave her part of the truth, afraid of what she'd think if she knew I'd been dreaming about her since before we met. How was that possible? "I don't know why. I'm sorry."

Her eyes went wide for a moment. "Oh," she said. But she didn't sound surprised; she sounded interested. "How did it happen?"

"The fault line, it was in my dream."

She sighed deeply. "It's getting worse. I thought they were going to send recon teams out to collect everyone that escaped, but all they did was bring in engineers to service the wall."

"What?" I asked, surprised. Figuring out how I'd dreamt of her before I knew her would have to wait . . . but, maybe I *had* known her before? She'd kissed me like she'd known me. It was just one more thing I didn't understand, and there were already too many uncertainties fighting for answers in my mind. What mattered now was that we were out. We'd escaped, but we weren't the only ones. "What about all the people that got out?" There had to have been over a hundred.

She shook her head and frowned. "They closed the Border. No one is getting back in or out. They don't want any of us returning."

The Heads of State had decided it was too much hassle to expend the resources on catching everyone, sending us to health facilities for vaccines because we were outside the Border and outside the protection of the Dome, and ultimately too much hassle to give a shit. My heart sank. Because of Eve and me, those people were destined to die unless they knew how to live off the land. Maybe there were still places left that were habitable, but they'd have to survive the desert first. Without food and without water.

What the hell had we gotten ourselves into?

I looked away from Eve and climbed up the side of the ravine, sliding a couple times as I tried to find my footing in the mixture of sand, rock, and dirt. When I made it to the top, I looked out across the barren land, back toward the Border. The section of the wall that had sparked blue and white earlier was completely sealed and glowed faintly blue like the rest of the nearly invisible Dome: a clear structure made up of hexagonal panels covering the Regime. It currently reflected the milky light of the moon. It was night inside and outside the Dome, but it felt like we were a world away from where we'd been mere hours before. My old life was gone, I realized, though I did not mourn for it.

"Are you okay?" Eve asked again as she climbed up next to me and lay down in the hot sand.

"I don't know what it means to be okay," I said truthfully. "How are you doing?"

"I feel the same way you do." She sighed. "I'm just glad I found someone who's like me." She smiled, and I did too. It was hard to think everything was changing for the worse when I saw that smile.

Her dark brown, almost black eyes watched me closely as I looked at the Dome, and I finally asked her what we were going to do. I'd always wanted to get out and see the world beyond the Border. Lying in the sand beside her, I understood I was in way over my head and completely unprepared for the harsh landscape and thick, dusty atmosphere. I'd seen the landscape I was lying in before from the Trams when they slowed down enough and you could get a glimpse of the world below instead of it just being a blur, but it seemed so different from above. Like a clip from an old documentary about Mars before the planet was destroyed by an asteroid and there were no more missions to the Red Sea. It hadn't seemed real. Now, it was very real and very dangerous.

But you're alive, Adam, don't forget that. I was alive, for the time being.

"How the fuck are we going to get from Las Vegas to Cincinnati?"

"Just let me explain, will you?" Eve said, a tinge of irritation in her voice.

We both stopped talking and instinctively ducked down as a Tram raced over us, the blue tracks gleaming as it did. Some Trams were allowed to leave the Dome for a short period of time to get to a destination quicker, like I said, but there were also Trams used solely by government personnel, and that included security agents and Officers.

I looked at Eve quizzically. "I thought they shut down the Trams?"

"They closed the Border, but they must still be sending agents and Officers out to look for those that escaped."

"I thought they didn't care."

"My guess is that they definitely do not care. I think it's more about appearances at this point."

I exhaled, and she pulled out her small bag from her jacket pocket as the Tram went back over us, heading for the Dome. She dumped out two of the remaining Monitors with the small earpieces still attached to them. "Here," she said and dropped one in my hand. "This should still work. If I'm not wrong, we're within range of the Border, and they keep the signal strong enough out here for those heading to the Edge."

The second I put the earpiece in and flipped a small switch on the Monitor to the "on" position—the same switch that would be permanently turned on in the brain—I heard a broadcast from downtown Vegas, the same one Linda always had on at the bar.

"This is Monica LaGrange reporting live from the Las Vegas station where hours ago, nearly two hundred passengers—mostly lower class citizens from the outskirts of the city—escaped through a break in the electric wall surrounding the Border. Here with me now is Director Derrick Madden, Head of Defense and Security (D&S) within Officer Region #106. Director, what can you tell us about the Monitors found near the breach in the wall?"

"Thank you, Ms. LaGrange. This is Director Madden speaking. The devices found near—"

I pressed a knob on the side of the Monitor, one that was generally controlled by brain waves, to switch the station. I was interested in what was happening around the Regime, not the place I'd just come from.

The voice of a distressed news anchor came through. "The rupture of the fault line in Cincinnati has triggered widespread plate movement across the Regime. We're getting reports from various cities about the appearance of new fissures. The major fault line near St. Louis has opened. Excuse me, ruptured. Yes, that's right, the New Madrid Fault Line has ruptured. The government has officially issued a 'Red Zone' alert for the Capital of the Regime. The Heads of State and the Head of Regime were evacuated from the city moments ago. If you are within the zone, your Monitor should have issued the evacuation order. Hold on, Kati, I think we're getting something in from Vegas." There was a brief pause. "The Hoover Dam is seeing major activity, and there are signs of cracking in the concrete at its base. Kati, are you hearing this?"

"Yes, Jim. This is Kati Dunabeck, Denver, and we have just been issued a 'Red Zone' for the area to the southwest of us. There is going to be major flooding in the Colorado River and—oh my god, Jim . . . Jim, the dam is collapsing! Jim—"

I yanked the earpiece from my head. *"Judgement . . . He's watching us . . ."* I thought about the words the woman had spoken at the station days ago. I didn't understand when she'd first said it, but I was remembering more and more from our discussion of religion in grade school. The Screens had shown us paintings of fire and pits of Sulphur, but it had seemed so far away from anything that was real. I thought about *The Last Judgement.* It had long since been erased from existence when the water levels rose and the Metropolitan Museum of Art was engulfed with New York City. There were still images of it, though, as there were of everyone and everything, and I pictured it clearly in my head. Behind a figure resembling a skeleton with wings, there lay the earth in ruin. Deep holes in the barren ground pulled people into the darkness below the wings of a skeletal figure—perhaps he was Death—and others struggled desperately for air among crashing waves in a deep blue ocean. In the distance behind the figures being pulled into the land and sea was a burning city. Flooding was taking place around the Regime, Cincinnati was on fire, and fault lines were splitting earth and triggering more quakes, landslides, and infernal cracks in the ground.

"Judgement . . . He's watching us . . ." I rolled the old woman's words over again in my mind. Did she truly believe there was someone of a higher power watching us, doing this to us? How could anyone let this happen? I was a cynical person; I knew that. Humans had nearly destroyed the planet we'd evolved on, but there were parts of it that were still breathtaking, and there were people that were still good, weren't there?

"It's going to be dangerous, but we have to get to Cincinnati," Eve said after a long period of silence while we both tried to cope with what we heard on the Monitors.

"You've said that," I pointed out, "but you haven't told me how we're going to get there."

"There's an engineering outpost to the northeast of us toward Salt Lake, but not that far. It's only about ten miles from here. That's assuming I can still get in. We'd also be assuming we could find supplies there. I know that's a lot to bank on. I do have a water bottle, at least . . ." She seemed to be losing faith in what she was saying. It was a lot of "ifs," but our world was literally going up in flames, so why not? I had nothing left anyway, except for the girl standing next to me that I barely knew.

"I'm in," I assured her. "I'll follow you wherever you lead."

That made her grin. "That's probably the stupidest thing you could do."

"No." I shook my head. "You know a lot more than I do about this, and you're much craftier."

"You mean I'm a good criminal?"

I laughed lightly. "No, I mean you're observant. You could survive out here. I wouldn't last a day alone. My only talent is being pessimistic."

"I like that about you," she said with another laugh. "I mean it." She grabbed my hand and squeezed it. I thought about the kiss at the station, and I looked at her lips longingly. I think she knew because she blushed and turned away before I could do anything about it.

I pushed myself off the ground and held my hand out to help her up. "Come on, thief. We've got an outpost to get—"

Before I could finish my sentence, I felt something hard hit my head. Stars swam before my eyes, and soon, my vision went completely black. I didn't even feel my body hit the ground.

CHAPTER 9

"How were you getting paid all those years, boy? Pretty little boss of yours paying you under the table? Oh, that's right. You were a bartender, weren't you? Living off tips. Well, you can kiss that goodbye. You and your girlfriend are dead."

At first, the pain screaming in the back of my head told me I wanted to be dead, but I knew deep down I didn't. I wanted to live, to figure everything out, but more than anything in this moment, I didn't want Eve to die. I looked over at her. Her hands and feet were bound, and there was a gag in her mouth. I clenched my fists and winced; they were tied together tightly with coarse rope.

"Fuck you." I spat at the security agent. "Fuck you and the fucking Regime. And what good are you to them anyway? You're stuck out here in this fucking wasteland with us, aren't you?"

Remember what I said about knowing what was right and what was wrong to say? That wasn't the right thing to say. But the piece of shit had followed me after the breach to personally take pleasure in erasing me from existence. He'd killed Linda and wanted to kill me.

"Your real last name isn't Krichmar, is it? I didn't want to believe that I was staring at a dissident, but oh was I. Now I'll have the pleasure of removing a lowlife with no Monitor"—he paused to glare at Eve—"and a criminal who caused a security breach at the Border from existence. Two birds with one stone, as they used to say." He finished with a deep, sick laugh. He was enjoying himself, and I expected that was why he didn't tie me up entirely as he had Eve. He didn't want it to be easy. He wanted a fight. I was probably going to lose, but I was going to give him exactly what he wanted.

I leapt from the ground and brought my tied hands up to smash the man in the face. I wanted to knock his helmet off and look into the eyes of the man who'd mercilessly killed Linda, but it didn't work. Not at all. Before I could bring my hands down on the helmet, his fist shot out and punched me in the ribs. None of them broke, but it sure felt like something had shattered inside my body.

I staggered backward but managed to stay upright while the agent inched closer and closer, a wide grin on his face. The anger I felt toward him for killing Linda rose inside me, making my blood boil. If only I could get my hands free, it would be an easy fight. I had a reason to live: to save people like Linda from those who'd lost their humanity.

Fighting against the throbbing pain from where the agent hit me, I gritted my teeth and raised my leg to try and kick him in the chest, but before I did, he dropped over. I stood awestricken at his limp body on the ground until I noticed blood running down the back of his neck and into his black uniform. My eyes shot to Eve, and I noticed her bound hands inside her small bag. She must have kept the control panel she stole from another agent: the one that set off the three Monitors.

I ran over to her and began untying her wrists. Once her hands were free, they shot up to her mouth and ripped off the cloth tied around her face to prevent her from making a sound.

"He should've been less worried about killing you and more worried about the girl with the ability to kill anyone with a Monitor." She was fuming. "Too bad he didn't stop to think about that. I guess old stereotypes die hard."

As she untied my hands, I said, "You're a genius. I'd be

dead without you."

I thought about it and realized she could've saved me getting punched in the ribs and saved herself from being tied up. "Why didn't you press it sooner?"

"I'm a criminal, not a murderer," she said matter-of-factly. She was more humane than most people I came across, including me.

Without thinking, I kissed her. Adrenaline coursed through me, and I didn't know how to control myself. It felt so good, so right, but I didn't know why.

She didn't stop me, and before I knew it, my hands were in her hair and my mouth was on her neck. My heart was beating so loudly, I was afraid she might be able to hear it. I tried to pull her into my lap, but she pushed away from me, breathing heavily.

"I'm sorry, Adam," she said in between breaths. "I can't. I'm sorry."

"Don't be sorry. You didn't do anything." What the fuck was wrong with me? "I know we have things we need to do. You're on a mission, and I don't want to take you away from that. I just . . ." I didn't have any excuse besides my increasing attraction to the girl who was a mystery to me.

"I know," she said. "I feel it too, but we can't be here. He has a tracker in his body." She pointed at the agent's limp form on the ground near us. Right, his Monitor was blown, but there was still the tracker that notified the Regime when a person was deleted from the registry of those who possessed Monitors. It was part of the identification chip. Someone was going to have to retrieve his body.

Before we left, we grabbed what the agent had on him: his black leather belt fit with his control panel, a nightstick, a Taser, a few weapons I didn't recognize, and a vile filled with a yellow liquid that Eve said was some kind of chemical weapon. We would've taken his money if he'd had any, but people didn't use physical paper anymore. That was inefficient when you had a Monitor. Electronic coins were traded for goods, and old paper money was only used on the black market. The identification chips implanted in our wrists were run over scanners to pay for purchases in store. Even that was growing old; most people chose to buy everything they needed digitally through the Monitors in their heads. I didn't have a Monitor, but technology was still a part of me. It was impossible to escape unless you were an Untouchable.

After we'd stripped the security agent's body of anything useful, I decided it benefitted us if I took his clothes as well. We didn't know how long we had before others showed up, but we took the risk. I pulled off my dusty jeans, flannel shirt that smelled faintly of hops, and tennis shoes that looked like I'd had them since I was thirteen, then quickly changed into the agent's shirt, vest, pants, boots, gloves, and helmet, all the shade of absolute darkness. I was thinner than the overly sculpted man who lay naked at my feet, but the clothes weren't too baggy. They looked like they were mine, and that was all that mattered if I was going to convince people I was a security agent.

I tried not to gag as I inhaled. The smell of blood inside the helmet was overwhelming. The air filtration system was working, just not fast enough.

"You look terrifying," Eve said. Her face wrinkled in disgust, and I noticed her hands clenched tightly at her sides. "I've always hated the uniforms. They make the agents look like lifeless creatures. I don't like not being able to see someone's face."

"I don't either, but I promise you I'm nothing like that man." I said the words but didn't quite believe them. I'd asked Eve why she didn't kill the man sooner, yet I'd run away after he killed Linda. I wasn't brave like her, not in the slightest.

"Do you think I can figure out how to make this thing work?" I asked and tapped the helmet when she didn't say anything. Every agent and Officer was fitted with a special helmet made for them alone. It held information on the people they suspected and were watching, as well as all the information about the Regime's Defense and Security systems. If I managed to turn it on, I'd have access to the inside of the Dome without being in it, as long as I was in range.

"There's a retinal scanner on the inside of the helmet's shield," Eve began. "The system only activates when their eyes are open. The minute they close, the system goes off. The only way that thing would work is if his eyes opened while the helmet was on. There's no way for us to access it. It's effective planning on Defense and Security's part. I just wish it wasn't."

I stared at her and was glad she couldn't see my baffled expression. Once again, she proved she knew about something that most people didn't. Only someone close to a person in Security, or someone who was in it themselves, would know that.

"How do you—" But she already knew what I was going to ask.

"My younger sister was a data engineer," she explained, but I felt like there was more to the story than she was letting on. "She worked on those systems."

"Why didn't you ask her to help you?" It was an ignorant thing to say, but I still didn't understand why she'd chosen *me*.

"She's dead, Adam. A pretty agent with a helmet like yours raped her, then accused her of attempting to access the classified information stored within the D&S systems she was working on. It all turned out well for him. Even got to finish her off himself."

"I—" I choked on my words. I didn't want to think that she'd been through something as horrible as I had with my mother, but what she described was infinitely worse. My mother took her own life to protect me. She would've eventually been killed by the Regime, so she didn't have a choice, but her death was by her own hands. I couldn't imagine living in a world where someone had killed my mother as easily as the security agent had killed Linda. Yet, that was real. That was Eve's world.

"I'm so sorry . . ." What could I say to her to make any of it okay? A handful of people who cared about me, or pretended to care, while I was at the foster home growing up had tried to tell me things about my mother like, "She's not suffering anymore." But I still suffered no matter how much they told me she wasn't. The things they said only made the fact that she was gone more pointed. I imagined it was the same way for Eve.

"It doesn't matter anymore," she said. She tried to sound indifferent, but there was pain in her voice. "She can't help—dammit!" Eve immediately pointed at the Dome. The lights at the station were flickering blue and white where a port would open and let out a Tram headed toward the Edge. But it wasn't going to the Edge this time; it was going to search for the security agent's body. No one had to tell us. We knew. We'd spent too long here. I should've known they wouldn't waste any time searching for one of their own, though I was shocked they cared enough to do that.

"Kara, look at this son of a bitch."

The woman let out a high-pitched laugh. "I hardly recognize him without the helmet," she said with another loud laugh. "Poor Hanson. I liked him better with it on, to be honest."

She stood next to a man the same height as her. If it weren't for her subtle curves, you wouldn't be able to tell the two agents were a man and a woman.

"I don't know," the male agent said. "He's got a nice body. I wouldn't have minded seeing him like this while he was still alive."

I lay close to Eve, gripping her hand tightly, as we hid behind a large grouping of boulders several feet away from where they stood above the agent's body.

"You're disgusting, Diego. Look at that hole in the back of his head. It's still oozing."

"That might be you if you don't watch your mouth around Amil."

"Shut up." Kara punched the other agent playfully in the arm. "Now help me pick up his body."

"Don't you want to send out a search for the sorry fuckers who took his clothes and weapons? They even have his helmet, Kara. That's a risk."

"There's no way to access any of its files. You know that."

"What about his weapons? The control panel?"

"Let them kill whoever they want out here. That's not our problem, is it? They'd be doing the idiots who escaped a favor and saving them from starvation."

"Fuck it," Diego said after a moment. "Let's leave his body too. We've got way more important things going on. Infrastructure is going down all around the city. The security systems are next if we don't start doing something about it."

"Again, not our problem. Like you would even know what to do. Your poor parents didn't want you to learn how to code. Ha! They taught you how to write instead. What a fucking waste."

"Come on," Eve whispered hurriedly as the agents climbed up the steps that had materialized down out of the Tram to the ground. "We need to get to the engineering outpost. I know someone there who can help us." It was likely a connection of her sister's, but I didn't stop to ask. As the tracks lit up and the blue lights raced back toward the Dome, we stood up and started running as fast as we could.

CHAPTER 10

Truth be told, I wasn't used to the physical exertion of running for longer than a couple minutes at a time. The Monitors performed routine fitness programs on the body, for which the person was either conscious or unconscious, depending on their personal preference. Obesity was one of the many problems of the past that had been solved by the Monitors' control of food intake and desire, thanks to the simple manipulation of brain waves. Only Untouchables who didn't have the implants were likely to gain weight. That was if they could find enough food to eat leisurely instead of eating out of necessity.

Because I didn't have a Monitor, I was one of those people who were at risk, and though I was poor, I was not an Untouchable. If I'd had the opportunity to eat and not worry about how much food cost, perhaps I would've been obese, though I would've needed to reduce my hours at the Back Door working for Linda to a fraction of what they were. I was barely ever at my apartment, but I didn't want to be there anyway, so it worked out for both of us while it lasted.

"S-stop," Eve said, out of breath, as we came to a halt behind an extremely old, rusted vehicle that looked like it had been there for decades. There was barely anything left besides a roof and some rods. I clutched the side of it to keep myself from falling over and grabbed at my sides that screamed with the pain of running for the past thirty minutes. My adrenaline had helped me get to where I was, but as soon as I stopped, I felt just how strenuous physical exercise was. My heart raced, and I heaved as I sucked in deep breaths.

"Be quiet," she warned me. "I didn't stop for nothing."

I looked around us. There were a few other cars, as well as the remnants of deserted buildings, one of which was probably a gas station. Below our feet was heavily cracked pavement through which desert shrubs were trying to grow. I expected Eve to have stopped because there were people nearby or because she took pity on me. Neither was the case. There were no people in sight. It was just the two of us, and though the moon was bright, there were plenty of places someone could be hiding in the shadows.

"Put your earpiece in," she said. "We need to check the Monitors. We haven't felt anything out here yet, and that concerns me."

"The Dome covers almost the entire Regime. If the earlier news report was true, it should be containing the flooding and fire. For now." The Dome was supposed to protect the Regime from what happened outside of it, but that also meant that it contained everything that happened on the inside, good and bad. Out here, outside its "protection," we were safe from the disasters they were desperately trying to control inside.

"You're right," she responded, "but what about the shifting plates? We're on the coast; there are faults running all over the desert. We should be feeling their effects, even outside the Dome."

I took the Monitor she gave me, quickly shoved the earpiece in, and switched on the device. Crackling came through, but that was it. "Are you getting anything from the signal you're on?"

"A little, but it's bits and pieces. We're getting farther away from the Dome, so it makes sense."

"Farther away? I thought you said there was an outpost near the wall?"

"There is," Eve said. "But the outposts were built far

enough away from the Border so people couldn't see them from the Trams. The Regime doesn't want to give people any ideas about leaving its little slice of the world."

"The signal should still be strong enough for the engineers and technicians, though, shouldn't it?" I asked. Or maybe the people that made sure the Dome didn't collapse weren't important enough to keep track of outside the Regime.

"It goes in and out. They have to chop it up to make sure that when people get out like we did, they aren't able to go on with life the way they're used to." Once again, she seemed to know everything. "My sister," she mumbled. "She taught me a lot."

"Wait," she started again. "I think I'm getting a broadcast from St. Louis. They're calling for flash flooding worse than that in Denver. Extreme thunderstorms are happening from there to the East Coast. Lightning just struck a woman crossing—"

"What about Cincinnati?" I asked, cutting her off. The entire Regime was a catastrophic nightmare, but she hadn't mentioned anything about the major fault line in the city that had triggered it all.

She clicked the small control on the Monitor to change the signal but shook her head. "Just keeps saying 'Red Zone,' and there are evacuation sirens blaring in the background. The reporters must have left the office. Maybe the fault line got another telecom building. If not, it must be really bad to make *them* leave."

"Eve," I said as I took a deep breath. "Eve, slow down. I c-can't keep running. I'm going to throw—" Before I could finish my sentence, a tremor shook the ground and sent me crashing to my knees. I winced as a sharp rock dug into my shin and the rough sand scraped my palms.

"It's got to be another fault rupturing!" Eve screamed, her voice shaking with the earth beneath us. "This is what they said happened with the first one!" She'd fallen to the ground beside me and held onto my arm with one hand. Her other hand clutched a Monitor. She already had the earpiece in, and her brows were scrunched together as she tried to listen to the choppy signal coming in from Las Vegas.

I looked to my right to see the Dome a couple thousand yards away. We still had two miles to go before we made it to the outpost, according to Eve. How she knew the exact route there from the Border Station, I was not yet sure.

As I looked at the Dome, I could see dark storm clouds whirling inside, almost as dark as a starless night. But that was the least threatening part of the natural disasters occurring across the Regime.

"How are the earthquakes not destroying it?" I yelled at Eve as I motioned to the Dome. It was getting hard to hear with the dust spinning and whipping around us, forming dust devils in the howling wind. The only light left outside was that of the moon. Without it, we wouldn't be able to see a thing.

"Earthquakes don't affect the Dome, remember?" she screamed back and tore out her earpiece.

"I know! But there have been several around the Regime! The plates seem to be shifting at a continuous rate, and what about everything else going on in there? How can the data centers sustain all of it?" There were several hundred thousand data centers around the Regime controlling the functions of the Screens, the Monitors, and everything in between. But what was happening didn't seem like anything that could've been predicted. The Dome itself was made of electric signals that created the appearance, feel, and safety of a real structure, but it would be destroyed as soon as the data centers collapsed.

"I don't know how it's all going to play out, but they didn't leave anything out of the equation when planning! I know that much!" Eve yelled. But this was something beyond what anyone could've imagined, wasn't it? We were prepared for another World War: one with humans, not Nature.

"It doesn't matter now, Adam. What we need to worry about is getting to the outpost and living to see another day!" With that, she pushed herself from the ground. I had to reach out and grab her arm to steady myself and her as I stood and another large tremor shook the ground.

"I know this hasn't been easy!" she continued. "But our bodies are stronger than you think, even without the Monitors! We just have a few more minutes and we'll be there, I promise!" She didn't have to convince me to go with her. I wouldn't have left her for anything, and I had absolutely nothing to begin with.

A minute passed before the tremors subsided, and I didn't bother putting in my earpiece to hear about the destruction of the city I'd left behind. I didn't want to hear about the collapsed buildings and the dead. I couldn't take any more of it.

It was another ten minutes before the wind died down, but we hadn't wasted any time. My sides hurt again from running, and I tried to control my breathing as I looked around. I was standing at the bottom of a hill leading away from the Dome. Eve stood to my left, staring at a wide-open space in front of us. I watched her skeptically. There was nothing around but cacti and a few desert shrubs and trees. Absolutely nothing.

"Eve?" I asked. There was probably still a ways to go before we found the outpost. That had to be it because I didn't see anything.

I squinted in the low light, and then, just like that, I caught a glimpse of something gleaming several feet above me. At first, it looked like something was caught in a tree and was reflecting the moonlight. Then I saw the small glint extending down from the initial point to form a straight line. I looked harder and could see that it extended not just vertically but horizontally as well, forming the outline of a right angle.

Eve had mentioned that the outpost was far enough away from the Dome that people would be less likely to run into it. She'd meant that they literally would.

I was looking at the building, though all I could see were the small silver lines reflecting the moonlight. It was completely invisible in the landscape, and anyone not looking hard enough wouldn't notice. It was a genius design, and it made perfect sense. I'd heard rumors throughout my life that the first Head of Regime ordered any buildings where classified work was carried out to be removed from public perception. The rumor was that the architects and data engineers working on redesigning those buildings had figured out a way to use reflective panels to create the illusion that nothing was there. Clearly, their designs had been a success.

Eve smiled as she gazed at the building. "It's amazing, isn't it?"

I nodded my head, mesmerized. "But how do you get in?"

She didn't answer my question. She only smiled wider and took a step closer until I assumed she was standing directly in front of it. Then she raised her hand, and a small panel with glowing white electric numbers ranging one through ten appeared in the air. She quickly typed in a five-digit combination, and a large black rectangle appeared in front of us, blocking my view of what had been a group of cacti. She'd opened the door. But how? It crossed my mind that her sister had probably worked here, and my heart sank again at her tragedy.

The minute we stepped through the ominous door into the building, it was as if we'd been transported to another world. Across the four walls of the giant, one-room complex were massive Screens that showed a seamlessly moving image of the ocean. A surround sound system made it sound as if we were standing on the beach. Waves crashed around us, and the caw of gulls filled the air. I gasped. That was a creature that had long been extinct.

That wasn't the only thing that was strange about the beach. The sand and water weren't littered with plastic and other trash like most pictures of the ocean were. The water was turquoise and crystal clear, unlike anything I'd seen before, and the sand was pure white and looked like powder. The electronic panels that made up the floor displayed an equally seamless image of the sand, making it look as though we were standing on the beach. I took a step forward, and the surround sound system mimicked the crunching of my boots on the sand. The panels even created footprints where my feet had been. These interactive systems were usually reserved for the elite members of society with enough money to craft their perfect world out of wires and projections.

"It's beautiful." Eve sighed as she looked around the room. "I wish my sister could have seen it."

Wait. Sister? "I thought she worked here . . ." My eyebrows drew together. "Eve, how did you know how to get in the building?"

She walked to the center of the room without a word, her feet crunching in the sand as she did, and waved her hand in the air when she stopped. A control panel immediately appeared beneath her palm. Images of blueprints and a continuous feed of running code automatically flashed to life on the screen.

"I lied to you," she said, her voice low against the rolling water and birds endlessly calling to one another.

"What?" I took a step toward her but was stopped as a swooshing sound broke the seamless loop of crashing waves.

Eve looked up from the control panel and jumped as a black rectangle appeared in the turquoise ocean and a figure stepped through the wall in front of her. It was a woman about the same age as Eve: somewhere in her mid-twenties. The woman's honey-blonde hair was cut in a sharp line at her jaw, and her wide eyes were as blue as the ocean rolling on the walls. She was holding an electronic tablet in her hands and dropped it as she entered the room and saw Eve standing in the middle of it. The device hit the floor with a soft thud, but nothing happened to the Screens. Technology was no longer fragile in that capacity.

The woman gasped. "Eve! What are you doing here?"

"I could ask you the same question, Aimee," Eve said. The way she spoke her name made it sound like a bad word. Eve laughed bitterly, then became angry. She threw her hands up and pointed at the Screens on the walls. "What the fuck is all this? Are you kidding me? People are dying, Aimee! People are dying, and you're out here in your own little bubble!"

"You have no idea what I've been dealing with!" Aimee snatched her tablet from the floor. There was an imprint in the "sand" where it had landed.

"This isn't real!" Eve screamed. "You can't hide in here!"

Aimee stiffened and turned to face the wall. "Show me Cincinnati," she whispered, sending a signal to her Monitor. For a moment, nothing happened, then the Screens erupted into chaos. The telecommunications building that had been the center of communication in the city was completely gone. Broken electric wires blazed across the streets, and a Tramway that connected to the building had collapsed into the earth with it.

"This used to be called the Cincinnati Arch," Aimee said, though you could barely hear her over the noise in the background. All the screams and sirens blared at once, but she never made a move to turn the sound off. "It was a fault that lay outside the center of the city. Now that the tectonic plates have shifted, it has destroyed everything there. I'd been telling Defense and Security for over a year that we were getting signals in that region, and they ignored me." She was quiet for a moment, letting the images sink in. "Or maybe you're not interested in this, Eve? Maybe you want to see more?" Aimee whispered another command, and the eastern coast of the Regime appeared. The engineering outposts outside the Dome were flooding, and people were drowning.

"You know NYC, Jersey, and D.C. all disappeared years ago with the rising water levels. The seismic zone that ran through that area, Ramapo, it didn't just disappear. It was hidden underwater. Look at it! It's causing tsunamis all along the coast. The Dome can raise the barrier of solid steel, but that might not be enough. If that barrier breaks because of the earthquakes or if the tsunamis get high enough, the cities along the coast are doomed. It's all happening too fast."

A flooded plain had an electric wire in it. A drone shot from above showed a man lying on a board, just waiting to fall in the water and die from electrocution. "See that man? He is one of our best data engineers on the coast," Aimee said, her voice cracking as she did. "But they're not sending anyone to save him."

She took a deep breath and collected herself. "Or maybe this is what you were looking for?" There was a tone of finality in the way she spoke, and as she looked at the Screens, the image of St. Louis appeared. The Capital. "The Head of Regime and the Heads of State are gone, of course, but what about everyone else?" She showed us a picture of the Mississippi River. "It's running backward again. This happened before, a long, long time ago. Look at it." The river was causing levees to break all along the banks of the Capital. "You know why they put the Capital there? Because of access to the water, for energy and electricity. It was the reason the city did so well, even before the Regime, or so we've been told. Now it's going to be the reason the people that can't get out of the city will die." I thought about the apartment building I lived in and the squalor around that neighborhood. I could only imagine what was happening to the lower classes living in the Capital.

Aimee finally turned around to look at Eve. "Don't tell me I'm pretending that nothing is going on. I've been here since this all started four weeks ago. But where have you been? Off stealing money from the elite and pretending to help the starving? What about all this? You could have come. You could have been here with me."

"You know I couldn't. Someone would have tried to kill me."

"Who?" Aimee screamed. "I'm the only one left here. The State moved the data, systems, and electrical engineers further north. The Cascadia Subduction Zone up there is causing major damage in the northwestern portion of the Regime. They needed all the help they could get, so they left me here."

Something washed by underneath my feet, drawing my attention away from Aimee and Eve to the hyperreal Screen below. It appeared I was standing near the edge of the Mississippi in St. Louis. As I looked down, a stuffed dog with fur matted from the water floated quickly past my feet and off toward the large port positioned along the river bank. I wondered for a moment if it would ever be used again.

Don't think like that, Adam. This can't be the end of everything. It wasn't, was it?

Everything felt like a mystery, and I was no closer to getting answers. What was happening to our world? Why had Eve brought me here, and why had she lied? Clearly, she and Aimee had been close, whether they were friends or just colleagues, and clearly, Eve *had* worked here, not her sister, which probably meant Eve was the data engineer. She knew the route to get here, knew the codes to get in, and she obviously knew how to run the systems. So why did she lie about her sister, if she even had one?

Something else washed by—a small, yellowed tennis shoe—and I was pulled from my thoughts. What the Screens were showing was real, even though it felt like I was glimpsing an alternate reality. I didn't want to look, but I couldn't stop myself.

I scanned the rest of the surroundings, but when I looked to the left, I immediately wished I never had. My heart stopped. "No," I whispered. My stomach twisted, and my breathing hitched. A young girl, maybe ten, lay motionless on her back. Water was rushing into her mouth and pulling her body toward the swiftly moving river to my right. If I was standing there in reality, the water would come up to my knees.

I couldn't pull my focus away from the girl. I no longer heard what Aimee and Eve said, if anything. The little girl's eyes were open wide, and there was a large burn mark on the left side of her face and body, singeing parts of her sweater and jeans. She looked *dead.*

Though I knew I was only looking at a projected image, I ran over to where she was, but the current was moving so quickly, by the time I got to her, her body was almost out of view of the Screens. I ran to follow her, pressing my hands up against one of the panels as I watched her float away. When I finally pulled back, black imprints of my hands proved that I was separated from the girl and could never save her. There were buildings on fire around the city. How did she get there? Why was this happening to people?

I winced as I thought about the pain the girl must have gone through. How much it must have hurt to be burnt like that.

The running water rushed past me, roaring as it did, but the uniform I wore never got wet. I wasn't there. I was in the desert, inside a building indiscernible to the eye, thousands of miles away from the Capital, and was utterly helpless.

"Who are you?" My body tensed with alarm as Aimee's voice sounded behind me. Though I never left the room, I felt like I was still in St. Louis, wishing I could take the little girl's place.

Aimee was standing extremely close to me, and when I turned around, she was holding a small device in her hand. A neural scrambling device. "The last time one of *you* set foot in here, you came to take away Eve."

I blinked, taken aback, then looked down at my clothes. She must still have thought I was a security agent. One of them had taken Eve? I wanted to ask about what happened, but Aimee took a step closer, pushing the weapon into my side, and though she didn't trigger it, anxiety raced through my body.

Her eyes narrowed to slits. "Tell me what you're doing here."

"Aimee, stop!" Eve shouted and rushed over. The surround sound system played the sound of splashing as she did. "He's not like the others, I promise! He's with me!"

Aimee didn't budge.

"I don't know what happened," I said slowly. I understood that they were upset and anxious; I was too. But there were much bigger problems. "Listen, I—"

Aimee pushed the weapon deeper into my side, and I tensed. She wasn't going to stop. "I'm not here to hurt anyone," I continued hurriedly. "I'm here because she led me here." I pointed a black-gloved finger at Eve.

Aimee looked back at her. "You led him here?" Her expression was full of confusion. "Why?"

"We've known each other for a long time," Eve said.

We've known each other for a long time. If she could see my face, she'd know I looked just as confused as Aimee. We'd just met. I barely knew anything about her, except that she'd lied to me about working for the Regime. But there was the dream . . .

"He's not a security agent, Aimee," she quickly went on. The blonde woman still made no attempts to put down the weapon. "Put. It. Down." Eve's tone was patronizing, more annoyed than worried. If I wasn't afraid of being shocked into unconsciousness, I might laugh. But I was afraid, absolutely terrified. More than that, I was angry. We were wasting time.

Aimee glared at me, her piercing blue eyes searching for a reason not to listen to Eve. Then, she slowly began to remove the weapon. "I don't care who he is, and I don't—"

"Stop!" I yelled. I was done. "Was I the only one that saw that little girl? Are either of you paying attention to what's going on out there? I'm here because I want to do something to help them!"

"Ha!" Eve exclaimed, surprising me, then said angrily, "Don't play the hero card, Adam. You wanted to run away from your life just as much as those people at the station who got through the Border. You wanted a fresh start."

"So did you," Aimee said, furious. "That's why you left me here in this fucking place. I needed your help."

"Don't start." Eve glared at her. "You know I had to leave."

My fists clenched. "It doesn't matter why any of us are here!" I was angry about what Eve said to me and angry that she'd lied, and I did want answers, but all that seemed pretty low in importance compared to people drowning in the Capital and dying all around the Regime. Arguing wasn't going to help anyone, and that was the whole reason I thought I'd been led here. I thought we were going to try and do something good.

I kept seeing that little girl's face, kept thinking about the old lady who died at the tracks, and my boss who was killed right in front of me out of hysteria. I felt my anger rising faster and faster. "We need to save these people."

"What if there's no saving them?" Eve asked, frowning. She no longer appeared upset or irritated, but lost.

She might be right, but I didn't want to believe it yet. "What are you talking about? You are the one who led us here! You're an engineer, you're a scientist—" I pointed between the two of them, and no one corrected me, meaning that I was right about Eve. "You both worked for the Regime! You must know of some way back in or some way to get those people out!"

Eve looked at me with her large brown eyes for a moment, then finally said, "I didn't know how bad it was."

"It's bad inside and out," Aimee said, her shoulders falling.

The image of the man lying on a board in the water came to my mind. How was it even possible to get everyone inside the Regime out without running into bigger problems once they crossed the Border? They'd drown. Or starve if they were in the desert.

There has to be a way.

Just then, the images on the Screens blinked out of existence, and the lights went black. A low tremble shook the floor, but it wasn't anything like Eve and I experienced earlier. I quickly dug the Monitor and earpiece that Eve had given me out of my pocket. I ripped off the helmet and threw it to the ground, causing a loud thud when it landed, and shoved the earpiece in. I flicked the Monitor on, but nothing happened when I did. We were still in range. We had to be for the Screens to be working at the capacity they were only moments ago.

"Eve?" I muttered. I could feel her moving closer to me. I was still angry and confused, but I had to let that go if I was going to get through this.

"Adam," she whispered. "I'm sorry about what I said."

"It's okay. It doesn't matter now. I tried the Monitor. Nothing's coming through. I think the broadcasts are down."

"I was afraid of that."

The lights came back on suddenly, but they were dim. Aimee looked around the room. "The Generator must be running." It was the Regime's backup power supply built on solar, water, and wind energy.

Aimee narrowed her eyes in concentration. "I'm not hearing anything from the stations."

"She still has hers," Eve explained, glancing at the Monitor still in my hand.

I didn't stop to think about what that meant. If the backup power supply was being used, that meant something bad enough had happened to shut down the main lines, and the Regime couldn't be completely sustained through other means, and if the Regime shut down, so would the Dome. Who knew how bad the disasters would get after that. "How much power is being supplied to the Regime through the Generator?" I asked.

"It's hard to say," Eve said. "I never worked directly with the engineers maintaining the system—I just worked on assignments for different sections of the Dome out here—but if we're getting power, that means that the Regime is still functioning on some level. I wish I had a better answer, but the power grid is a complex machine, even for me."

Eve had walked over to the center of the room where she'd been when we first entered the building and waved her hand. The desk with the code continuing to run sprang back on. I felt completely removed from everything that was happening. I knew the basics of artificial intelligence and computer programming, but I was so far outside the technological realm Aimee and Eve were operating in.

I wanted to know more about this girl who said she'd known me for a long time. I tried to rack my brain to remember kids I'd gone to school with, but no one came to mind. As far as I remembered, the first time I'd seen her was at the tracks in Vegas. I remembered her staring at me like she'd seen a ghost.

"This is the data warehouse for the Dome," Eve

murmured as I walked closer to her, and she pointed at the code. I couldn't understand the letters, dashes, and random numbers, but it all meant something important to her. I wished I could wrap my brain around it.

She swiped her hand left across the screen, and another program came up. "Most of the data strictly concerns the functions of the Dome, and Aimee has access to seismologic and geologic data, but I know enough to hack into the signal database to get information on Trams, autonomes, and most telecommunications. Unfortunately, we don't have access to the Monitors," she continued, "or anything to do with them at all. If I had that access, I would turn them off immediately."

Aimee's face screwed up. "Turn them off? I don't think our brains would be able to function without them. It would either kill us or people would go insane without the stimuli. It would only augment the hysteria."

"Maybe one day we'll know just how bad it would be," Eve said softly, still concentrating on the program running in front of her. "The systems are continuing to adapt and function along the West Coast, but the northwestern and eastern sides are failing. Do you know if anyone at the outposts along that side is still there? Any of the systems or electrical engineers? We need them over there." Her voice sounded strong, but there was urgency and worry mixed in.

My heart beat faster and faster as I listened to them. But what could I do? I was just a bartender.

I made my mind up after a minute and left the dark room with black walls and floors reflecting our bodies instead of the images of catastrophe that were taking place around the Regime. I hated feeling useless and couldn't shake the image of the girl no matter what I did. I needed air.

I stepped through the black door that appeared in the wall in front of me, and once I was out, turned around, almost to check and see if anything had changed. The building's material still reflected the surroundings, rendering it invisible. I looked up to the roof and could see the thin line of light from the moon telling me that I wasn't hallucinating.

I'd grabbed the security agent's helmet before I left and quickly put it back on, leaving the earpiece in under it, hoping to hear something, but all I got was buzzing. With the Monitor tucked in the collar of the agent's black shirt, I made my way up the small hill to where I saw the Dome far off in the distance. Its hexagonal exterior was still intact, from what I could tell, but I doubted it could last as long as everyone hoped. It was meant to take us into the next centuries.

I thought about the electric structure longingly for a moment until I realized that I was outside of it and nothing was wrong with me. I wasn't ridden with disease or being struck by lightning; everyone was taught to believe that what lay outside the Dome was a toxic waste exposed to the harsh natural elements and all the illness we'd worked so hard to eradicate. But the danger wasn't necessarily outside the Dome. Sure, there were dangerous wild animals outside that had been removed altogether from the "sanctum" of the Regime, as well as poisonous water and food sources, but inside, people were still dying and still starving. If only we could get everyone out here . . . But how safe were we at the outpost, in the middle of the desert? There wasn't enough food or drinking water, though there could be if the Head of Regime ordered it, and even though there wasn't flooding like we'd seen through the footage of the East Coast, we were experiencing the earthquakes, same as inside the Dome.

Was there anywhere for people to go, really? What was the better choice? Stay inside and wait to see what happened, or try to get out? Generally, people thought of the Dome as a safe haven. Utopia was a word that was thrown around a lot by the Head of Regime and Heads of State. Alongside the Dome, our major advancement in society, supposedly, had been the creation of the Monitor system. It allowed us to do everything we needed, and it regulated our diet, fitness, and overall health. The people that didn't possess that technology were thought to suffer because of it. The Untouchables were always denigrated by society and the media, but who were we to say that they were living in any worse condition than the rest of us? People with Monitors still cheated, lied, and murdered. The Monitors were capable of controlling the brain's limbic system and stabilizing emotions, but the brain was also capable of evolving to meet that roadblock. The creation of an internal, forever-functioning machine developed from the desire to overcome the excessive violence and criminal behavior of our past. The Monitors helped, but they didn't quite work the way they were purported to. Nothing ever truly did.

And now that these disasters were taking place, what were the Monitors doing to help? They weren't getting people to safety, and they couldn't stop people from being electrocuted, burned to death, or drowning. They were useless. But was Aimee right? Would getting rid of them now only make things worse? I no longer knew what to think. Everything had been turned on its head.

"Red Zone statuses for all cities in the Regime will remain in effect—" The crackling of radio waves ceased, and a man's voice came frantically over the broadcast, then it stopped again. I flipped the Monitor on and off, and still nothing. I left it on and waited. A minute passed, then the man's voice came back through. "This is Amir Ephron reporting live from Topeka. We are experiencing intermittent blackouts across the Regime, but the Generator is running, and we're expecting a full-power reboot within the next twenty minutes. I repeat, a full-power reboot in the next twenty minutes. The Red Zone status for the Regime is still in effect from east to west. We are working to collect civilians along the coast working in our critical outpost stations. Remain where you are, and you will be located. The activity along the fault zones in the East, and especially in Cincinnati, has ceased for the time being. We are waiting for confirmation from our scientists, but we advise everyone to remain in shelter until it is safe."

I ran down the hill and inside the building as quickly as I could. I had to get to Eve and let her know that help— whatever terror the Regime considered help—was on the way. She'd mentioned something about being killed if she were to be discovered here. I had no idea what she'd done to deserve something so horrific, but I wanted to believe I could save her if no one else. I didn't want to get my hopes up after listening to the broadcast that the nationwide disaster was over and that our people would be okay, eventually, but if Eve and I were safe, maybe we'd be able to help them.

"Eve! The radio! The Regime is sending search and rescue teams to the outposts surrounding the Dome to look for survivors!"

"I know!" Eve yelled back frantically, still standing at her station in the center of the room. "Aimee's been receiving the alerts. They already know she's here."

My heart thudded wildly. I'd forgotten about what Eve had said: Aimee had a Monitor, which meant Eve and I weren't safe.

Suddenly, I was aware I was wearing the uniform of the man she'd killed. Besides that, I was impersonating an agent, a crime in and of itself. I felt sick, but I couldn't start freaking out.

"They knew I was lying when I said there weren't other people here with me . . ." Aimee looked pale. "The Officers stationed at the response headquarters might even be listening right now."

Eve held up her hand, signaling Aimee to stop talking. "I can't concentrate. Just be quiet until I finish."

I watched Aimee intently. If Officers were surveying what she said and heard—which they could easily do thanks to the built-in criminal assessment components in the Monitors—I needed to remain aware and not say anything to give myself away. The Officers wouldn't know that Eve and I had killed the agent. How many hundreds of others had broken through the Border? Anyone could've done it . . . But I was wearing a security agent's uniform, a uniform that didn't belong to me and whose helmet didn't work. There would be no way for me to confirm I was an agent, but they wouldn't know I was impersonating one or that there was even an agent here. The

Officers could only hear and see what Aimee did, if they even cared enough to waste time on it. Why would they be alarmed? I was sure they had other problems to deal with. Even the agents that had come to collect the man that murdered Linda had said that there were way bigger things to worry about. They'd left his body because of that; again, it was more likely that they didn't care. Either way, I needed to calm down.

I took a few deep breaths, my eyes still on Aimee. It killed me to know that she could have her thoughts intruded upon like that, but what choice did she have?

My eyes flickered over to Eve. She must have had a Monitor when she worked here; there was no way to get a government job without one. I wondered if she'd had to get rid of hers because of what happened, then winced, thinking about the pain of going through the extraction surgery as an adult. The surgeons numbed people, but they never quite stopped the splitting headaches that came afterward, especially since the procedure was illegal and buying pain medication in a large enough dose was highly suspicious without a doctor's approval, which they didn't readily give out for fear of being caught. One had to rely on getting the drugs from nontraditional sources, like the Untouchables. Even though the pain was unbearable, most people refrained from stooping "so low." The procedure was also incredibly high risk, especially the older the person was. I was lucky I didn't remember going through it.

"There," Eve said at last, breaking my train of thought. "It looks like the search and rescue team they're sending out here doesn't have any security agents or Officers assigned to it. They're probably all on call around the major Border zones, especially after what happened in Vegas."

I let out a long sigh of relief, and Aimee's eyes lit up like she finally understood what had happened, but she didn't say anything in case someone was listening. She looked between Eve and me, and Eve nodded her head. Aimee finally knew the reason we were able to get to her; there would've been no other way for us to get to the outpost. Only individuals who worked at the outposts, or those with special permission like the agents and Officers, could ever leave the Dome. For everyone else, the only hope was finding a way to break through it, and most people died trying.

Even if Aimee's sensory inputs and outputs were under surveillance, I was at least comforted by the fact that her memories couldn't be tapped. It was against the privacy laws of the Regime, though I heard there was a bill sent up to the Head requesting that Officers and security agents be given complete access to subjects' memories and thoughts to minimize deviancy. No news on whether that would pass or not, but approving it and going through the process of rewriting a major part of the Monitors' program seemed like it came second to the possible collapse of our society.

The Monitors already had the capability to access specific memories and brain functions when an individual experienced extreme trauma or tried to commit suicide, but outside of those cases, it was forbidden. Or so we were told. I didn't want to take the chance. Then again, Eve had a security agent's weapon she'd already used to take another's life. With the press of a button, she could kill anyone with a Monitor. The small weapon belonged to a faulty system that banked on the fact that people rarely ever attacked agents and Officers and therefore didn't steal their weapons. Usually, people that did were killed, and their families became social outcasts. Those two things were typically more than enough to deter a citizen of the Regime from engaging in such an offense. After all, humans designed Monitors to increase their health and life expectancy, and they did most everything else to uphold or achieve a high social status.

Even though I knew Eve had the agent's weapon, could we justify killing people with the press of a button? Was that not as merciless as the man, whose clothes I stole, killing Linda without a second thought?

Sometimes it's about the bigger picture.

But how far were we willing to go for that? We'd seen wars

and had thus become closed off from the rest of the world, maintaining the Regime through no means but our own. World War IV had weakened us, and we lost nearly 40% of the population, although there remained around 12 billion. There were people everywhere, all the time, but it wasn't like it was before. Perhaps the chance of accessing or stealing a weapon like the one Eve took from the security agent meant that people continued to die, and the population's growth was regulated.

I watched Eve as I thought. Her fingers were continuously typing, moving so rapidly I barely saw them after a while. There was a deep crease between her brows from concentration, and her lips were pursed into a thin line. I hoped she was able to get us out of here so I could feel her lips on mine again. I hadn't forgotten about our moment in the desert. Was it simply out of fear and confusion? It couldn't be just that. I'd been attracted to her the moment I saw her at the Border Station, and I still felt it, even though she'd lied to me. Something told me she had a reason to do so. Then there was the dream. I'd dreamt of her before I saw her standing there, staring at me while thousands of people rushed around us to their different Trams, but I couldn't remember meeting her before that. Yet, she said we'd known each other for a long time. Who was she?

Eve looked up from her work and back at me. She wasn't able to see my eyes, but maybe she felt me staring at her from underneath the helmet. After a moment, she motioned for me to join her in the center of the room.

My footsteps echoed in the quiet space as I made my way to her, and when I reached the desk, she lowered her voice and whispered for only me to hear.

"You're going to pretend to be that security agent," she said, pointing at the uniform I was wearing. "They won't ask you for identification. They won't even have the information about his death. The rescue teams don't have access to that, only the security agents and Officers, though they'll be armed and ready to subdue us if they start to get suspicious."

I nodded my head, and she continued, "I don't know if the media already broadcast the footage from the Vegas station and figured out that I was involved in the breach, but I'm hoping the team coming here hasn't seen it. Either way, I need you to call me by another name. It's on my chip. I had it rewired after I left this job so I was no longer Eve. Call me Ara, okay? That's the name I've used to stay hidden. Aimee already knows. I'll explain everything after the team reaches us, I promise. We only have a few minutes."

She pointed at the computer screen in front of her. A GPS appeared with a red dot moving quickly toward our location. "I tapped into their autonome's signal system so I could understand what to expect. They might know Aimee wasn't telling the truth about being alone, but we can play that off. Everyone is under a lot of stress right now, especially people like her whose job it is to get whatever's happening under control."

I nodded again. It was a lot to take in, but I'd have to make it work for all our sakes.

"Ara?" I said her alias aloud. It wasn't "Eve," but I could manage. What I didn't understand was why she'd used her real name with me to begin with. She didn't know everything about me; she didn't know I wouldn't reveal her.

"Why did you use your real name when I met you?"

She rolled her eyes. I knew I should've waited to ask her, but I didn't know if I'd ever have that option again. She took a deep breath. "I knew I could trust you, Adam. I know that doesn't answer your question the way you want, but I promise I'll explain more later. We don't have much time. We need to act as calm as we can, given the circumstances. We can't be caught. Once we get back to the city, we'll be let go, if I'm not wrong. They don't know I used to run the software maintenance for this region. They don't know to ask me for help. Aimee, on the other hand, will have to stay. We could use her help, but I don't see how we'll manage to get away with her."

Eve typed a number and letter sequence into the screen,

then said, "Look at this." She pointed to a three-dimensional rotating map that appeared next to the running program. "This is the Tram leading to Cincinnati." It was a blue line reaching from the center of the city to the outlying territory and eventually connecting to other routes leading east, west, north, and south. "This line isn't running. The city is closed off to arrivals." Then she looked at me with intent in her eyes. "That is where we need to go. We need to be at the center of this. We need to figure out what we're dealing with. If we get close enough to an access point to the Tram, I can get it running again. I can overwrite its signal and keep the transportation services in the dark for a little bit. I still have the overwriting access codes memorized." She grinned in satisfaction. "I memorized a lot of things I shouldn't have."

I smiled and thought about all the important work she did that no one recognized her for anymore. She shouldn't need to hide it. She also shouldn't have to figure this out on her own. I was here, but what help was I? She needed Aimee.

"If you need Aimee with you, I'll make sure it happens and we aren't separated. I'll figure out a way."

Eve raised an eyebrow. "You will?"

"I'll try. We have that weapon, after all."

She frowned and said, "I don't want to use it ever again, but if we have to . . ."

I took her hand and squeezed it to comfort her.

She smiled half-heartedly. "Now, pretend you don't know me. Pretend I'm Ara." With that, she dropped my hand, and I heard the loud hum of a motor outside the building.

I thought back to the agents that had come looking for the body of the man that had killed Linda. They'd called him by his last name. I didn't have time to think of anyone else to impersonate. Any agent or Officer would find out I was lying no matter what name I chose. My anxiety overpowered my anger at the thought of the man. "You're Agent Hanson," I whispered to myself and turned to face the entrance of the invisible outpost, my heart pounding madly in my chest.

CHAPTER 11

As soon as Aimee received their signal, we exited the building through the black hole in the wall. An autonome was stationed feet from the entrance, a team consisting of two medical and one safety agent standing alongside its sleek, rounded body. The agents were all men around my age: in their early twenties.

"Aimee Jennings?" the safety agent asked. Unlike the security agents at the Border, these men weren't threatening and didn't wear coal-black helmets to hide their faces.

"Yes," Aimee said hesitantly at first, then quickly answered, "Yes, that's me."

"And you two?" The medical agent with dark skin looked at Eve and me. He didn't sound accusatory, just skeptical. "We weren't notified there were others."

They weren't notified? Was communication that broken within the agencies? Or were their employees stretched that thin? My guess was both.

I glanced down at the men's waists instinctively. Each agent was fitted with belts including weapons like the ones the security agents carried—the ones Eve and I possessed—though theirs weren't as deadly. Still, I felt uneasy.

"We should have been notified if there was a security agent with you," the man continued, his eyes fixed on me.

Fear twisted my stomach, but instead of giving in to it, I

pushed it away and straightened up where I stood. "Yes," I said, deepening my voice enough to sound commanding. "We just arrived before the call was put out to collect civilians from the outposts. I sent a signal through the Monitor system, but it must not have been delivered because of the outage."

If there was one thing I was good at besides mixing drinks and being pessimistic, it was lying. I learned how to convince people I was normal growing up, that I was a part of a society I wanted nothing to do with.

The man with the dark skin nodded, and I exhaled slightly in relief. "We've been experiencing that problem throughout the Regime, sir."

Sir? I didn't care if it was seen as too informal for a security agent; I wouldn't allow anyone to call me "sir." We were equals. Not all security agents were as self-centered and heartless as the man Eve killed. "Call me Hanson," I said.

"I'm Avery," the man with dark skin replied and stuck out his hand to shake mine before turning to Eve. "Did you arrive here with Hanson?"

"Yes," she said assuredly, then turned an outstretched wrist over for him to scan her identification chip.

"No need," he said.

"We're just happy to see you all alive," the other medical agent with green eyes and freckles covering every inch of his skin added.

"We've seen so many people who," the safety agent began, then paused. "Who aren't with us anymore." His voice cracked as he spoke. I imagined what they'd seen and thought sorrowfully of the little girl. I'd only experienced the disaster from the Screens, not firsthand.

"It's a living nightmare in there," Avery said, glancing back in the direction of the Dome. "We want to make sure we can help as many people as possible."

The man with freckles nodded. "Are any of you hurt?" he asked as he pushed his red hair from his eyes.

"No," Eve said. "We've experienced some tremors, but nothing like what's been going on inside the Dome."

"Have you all been outside long?" the safety agent asked. He had shoulder-length blonde hair and deep brown eyes. He was handsome, much like the others. Another advancement in our society was the elimination of what was generally considered unattractive. I heard the word used, but I didn't even really understand what it meant.

I drug myself back to reality. Was this man suspicious that Eve and I hadn't experienced what was happening under the Dome?

"I was on a Tram to the Edge when an earthquake hit a couple days ago and the tracks collapsed," Eve said hurriedly. Hopefully, they wouldn't know that such a collapse never happened. "Hanson was on the team that came and collected survivors. I didn't want to go back—couldn't go back, knowing I could try and help save people trapped out here without resources. Then everything started happening so quickly . . ."

"And here we are," Aimee finished gloomily.

"What is your position?" Avery asked. I hated that they were asking questions. We could already be on our way to Cincinnati by now, but I had to stay calm.

"I'm the acting geologist and seismologist for this region," Aimee explained.

"That is the skillset we need more of," he said, then went on, "We need to get you all back inside the Regime as soon as possible. The evacuated members of your team, Aimee, that were sent to the Northwest are on their way back and are regrouping to discuss precautions and steps forward. The Head of Regime has discussed air evacuation for major cities if we have enough time between the quakes and fault ruptures. It's too dangerous for people to stay."

But where were people supposed to go? There was the offshore holding in New Anchorage, but there wasn't enough space for everyone.

"It's too dangerous whether we have enough time or not," Aimee said, and I agreed. Why were they waiting?

"What about the Untouchables?" I asked without thinking.

Would someone of Hanson's position care about their survival? The Untouchables weren't able to be tracked like individuals with Monitors, but someone needed to try and save them just like everyone else, right? Something inside me told me the answer was "no."

"The Untouchables that were contacted have refused aid," the safety agent said with a sigh. "As far as we know, anyway. There was a small outbreak of their people at the Border in Vegas once they realized what had happened with the explosion at the Tram station. It was a frenzy in there, people running everywhere. They easily got in and out the Border."

He looked around nervously after he said this. "You think any of them would've gotten this far?"

The stigma against their people was so ingrained within our society, it was hard to tell if he feared what they might be able to do to him or was just scared of the rumors that were perpetuated through the media.

"They wouldn't want anything to do with us even if they did. Wouldn't even want our medicine," Avery put in.

Lie, I thought. The Untouchables wouldn't bother us because they'd be afraid of losing their lives.

"We've got to get going, Cal," the safety agent said to the red-haired man with freckles.

Cal turned to Eve, Aimee, and me. "You'll be with us until we reach Las Vegas. Then the three of us will be heading back out to search for more survivors at the outposts. Aimee, your job will be to meet up with the rest of your team. I hope you can find an answer."

A shadow of doubt cast across Aimee's face, but she gave him a weak smile. "I hope we can too."

"Do you know if any individuals from my squadron will be present?" I asked. I crossed my fingers and hoped that no other security agents or Officers would be at the facility they were taking us. If so, there would be no way to escape without killing them or ending up dead ourselves.

Cal only confirmed my fears. "There are several Officers at our headquarters to make sure nothing gets out of hand.

Everyone is under a lot of stress right now, and people are frantic to find their families."

"They'll be happy to see you come back alive," Avery added.

"Great," I said, trying to sound as pleased as I could. They'd know in an instant that I wasn't Agent Hanson. The other agents would be able to tell that the helmet I wore wasn't receiving signals or running like it would for a real security agent. Beyond that, I didn't know if the agents who'd found the man's body in the desert outside the Border notified anyone he was dead or just left him there instead of having to deal with his body. They didn't seem to care about him, but that didn't mean they wouldn't have upheld the law in some way. If they'd notified the security administration, then there was surely an alert in the system that his uniform and helmet had been stolen. They'd know. More than likely, they'd kill me before I, or Eve, ever had a chance to use the man's weapon in defense.

"I'm ready to give a full report," I said, though my stomach churned and my throat felt tight.

Just breathe, Adam. Just breathe.

With that, we climbed into the autonome. Eve and I sat down next to one another, the three men in the front and Aimee with us in the second row. The machine received a signal from one of the agents' Monitors and began driving rapidly back to the Border. Though the autonome had physical wheels, it felt as though we were gliding above the ground. If I weren't terrified of being caught and losing my life once we made it back to the city, I'd be interested in the complex machine that drove us without anyone lifting a finger. I'd never been inside one before. They were extremely expensive and reserved for individuals like Cal and Avery whose work required the ability to get places quicker than public transportation allowed. My work definitely did not necessitate that. Most people's did not. If everyone could afford an autonome, we'd constantly be stuck in traffic and never get anywhere.

The machine had a sleek and simple yet luxurious design, but I barely paid attention to anything except my own shaking hands. Once we were settled and no one was looking, Eve grabbed mine and squeezed.

Just breathe, Adam. Just breathe.

After a minute or two of silence, Cal spoke up, "Ara, what made you want to get involved with helping? I'm just curious. It's our job"—he motioned to himself and the two men sitting next to him—"something that gives us closure, but it's always interesting to see why others decide to help." Generosity was never anyone's strong suit in the Regime, especially toward people outside their family and social circle.

"I don't want people to die," Eve replied.

Aimee bowed her head. "The images that were projected on the Screens . . ." She didn't need to say any more. We all knew how horrific it was and dreaded how much worse we expected it to become.

"I watched my mother die," I said softly when no one else responded. Eve and Aimee stared at me. Tears formed in the corners of Aimee's eyes, and Eve squeezed my hand again. It was comforting, and I never wanted to let her go.

"I'm so sorry," Cal whispered as he looked back at me.

Maybe I was insane to mention something so personal, but I had a plan. If we befriended these men and made them trust us even a little, then maybe they'd sympathize with us. Maybe they'd help us.

"That was a long time ago," I continued. "Before the power outage, we saw something projected on the Screens from a drone in the Capital. It was a little girl; I'm pretty sure she was dead. She was floating in the water, and half of her body was burned severely . . . She'll never have a chance to grow up, to experience life. My mother made that choice for herself, but the people who are dying because of these natural disasters—the earthquakes, the tsunamis, the fires—these people don't have that choice."

The men in the front seat exchanged looks, then the safety agent, who Cal called Miles, said, "My husband got caught in a fire in a communications building in the Capital." His voice broke as he told us that his husband had been a reporter at the center. He was one of the men that we would've heard over the Monitors in the emergency broadcasts. "He refused to leave because he wanted to keep people informed about the disasters." Miles quickly swiped a tear from his face. "He was a great man. I just want to do right by him and help as many people as I can."

These men—Cal, Miles, and Avery—were suffering just like we were. They were no longer agents. They were human beings. My plan was working, though we were almost back to the city. We were heading farther north of the Border point where Eve and I had escaped, to another entrance for security, safety, and other response personnel with autonomes. I needed to act quickly if I was going to save Aimee, Eve, and myself.

"There has to be a way we can help you men," I started. "We're not interested in going back to our old lives; at least I know I'm not. I just want to help. I'll never be able to defend the city again if there are no people left to protect."

Eve and Aimee agreed.

"These phenomena are more serious than anything we've dealt with in our history," Aimee said. "I need to be out in the field monitoring the plates' movements. We can't contain what will happen; it's impossible, even with our technological advances. We never have been able to control nature, and I'm a firm believer that we never will be able to, but we can try to mitigate the loss of human life."

As Aimee spoke and explained the importance of tracking the movements of the tectonic plates below the Earth's surface in real time, Eve looked up at me and gave a hopeful grin. It wasn't the plan she'd envisioned, but it might be a way to save a lot more people, as well as ourselves.

"Would it be possible to get to Cincinnati?" she interjected.

Cal pushed his hair from his eyes again as he thought. Eve had just proposed something that was much more dangerous than him and his team going to search for more survivors along the western Border, but if their goal was to help save lives, maybe they'd see the good in going to the city where it all began. "It would be dangerous . . ."

"And the Trams in and out of the city are still shut down for the time being," Avery added.

"But we have this autonome. We could reprogram the system's course. We'd be safe in here, theoretically. Plus, there are so many outgoing search and rescue missions that, frankly, we're probably not even on anyone's radar," Miles said.

"It's risky," Cal murmured, looking at his colleagues, searching for an answer.

"This machine has the capability to expand, correct?" I asked. We were getting closer and closer to the machine's entrance to the Regime. We needed to decide.

Thankfully, Cal saw where I was going with the question. "We could bring back as many people as we could."

"A bus full, potentially," Avery said, enthusiasm building in his voice.

"And we could notify other teams about groups in critical condition near the epicenter of all this, or we could help them find safety, if that even exists anymore." Miles's tone was bleak.

"Don't talk like that," Cal said. "We can't lose hope."

"Will you please help us do this?" Eve asked, urgency in her voice. "Our people need help."

From the GPS on the machine's dashboard, I could see that we were only a hundred or so feet away from our current destination.

Avery cursed, then hurriedly waved his hand along the dash. A screen similar to the one Eve had accessed at the outpost appeared. A continuously running program and blinking input section awaited his next move.

"Are you sure about this, Ave?" Miles asked.

"Our goal is to save people, and that is exactly what we are going to do." With that, he punched in a set of coordinates manually and looked back at the three of us. "I hope you know what you're getting us into."

I looked out the window of the autonome. The light-blue glow of the electric structure that comprised the Dome was so close, its giant panels reached as far as I could see into the night sky above. The machine turned sharply to the left, and soon, we were going so fast, everything was just a dark black and brown blur.

Maybe we should've spent our time discussing what was going to happen once we got close to Cincinnati, but there was no way of knowing what was really needed until we were there and able to figure out the best course of action. The farthest we got was deciding we were going to stay in an adjacent city outside the epicenter of the fault, just in case. Aimee told us she believed it was only a matter of time before we felt the effects of the shifting plates again, though she said she could never be 100 percent certain. I hated not knowing, but it made every moment feel more vibrant and real. I felt like I'd been sleepwalking through my life, trying not to get noticed and biding my time until someone found out I didn't have a Monitor, and I was sent to a detainment facility, killed, or banished from society to live with the Untouchables. Since the day at the station when the old woman chose her death and I first saw Eve, everything shifted. Suddenly, I wasn't just Adam living in a shitty apartment on the shitty side of the city, dealing with people attempting to drink away their problems every night at the bar. Thanks to the Monitors, most people apart from the Untouchables never engaged in illegal substance abuse. Alcohol was as far as they got. It was one thing we never seemed to be able to live without. Including me.

A couple years ago, I spent several months lying in drunken delusion after leaving college until Linda found me at the Back Door, her wonderfully wretched bar, and took pity on my soul. She knew I wasn't normal, but she never said anything. She just helped. Then they took her away.

I watched Eve as she looked out the window of the autonome and wondered if she was thinking about someone she lost that was close to her. Then again, maybe she wasn't like me. I said that everything felt more vivid, not knowing how much time I had left, yet I couldn't stop living in the past.

Attempting to focus on the present, I tried to take in every detail I possibly could about the mysterious girl with olive skin and smooth dark hair that fell over her shoulders like silk. There were hints of freckles along her nose, and the longer I looked at her eyes, I noticed they weren't just dark brown but were ringed with green and golden flecks around her irises. The blue light in the interior of the self-sustaining machine gave Eve an otherworldly glow, making her deep-set eyes look even bigger in the shadows.

Her long, slender fingers tapped nervously on her jeans, and her chest rose and fell at a heightened pace. She was so fearless, but she was also afraid. This girl who led me away from the life I would've died leading had been through so much. I hoped we had the time to talk before chaos erupted again. I wanted so desperately to know who she was and why she had to hide her identity and live as Ara. Why did she have to give up her position as the data engineer at the outpost and leave Aimee behind? Why did she tell Aimee she'd known me for a long time?

Suddenly, something occurred to me. It was the tapping. The image formed in my mind immediately.

"You have to stop doing that. You're making me nervous," I'd said in my slow, drunk voice.

The girl had withdrawn her hand from the counter at the bar and shoved it under her leg where she sat on a stool next to mine. She was staring intently at her beer, and tiny beads of sweat were forming at her temple. She was so beautiful . . .

I couldn't believe I'd forgotten. The first time I saw Eve wasn't at the station. It was at the Back Door a week after I left college, or dropped out rather. I was one of the few people that ever did. I remembered wondering why a beautiful girl was at a bar in the middle of the day.

The girl hadn't made eye contact with me at first, and I'd been nervous she wasn't interested in talking to me. I should've been able to tell that. Clearly, she'd been focused on something else.

"A-are you okay?" I'd managed to say with minimal stuttering. "You seem—"

"What?" she snapped but still didn't look at me. "I seem what?"

"Upset," I said cautiously. "And h-hurt."

"Great," the girl muttered, and tears swelled in her eyes, but she blinked them back, taking a deep breath as she did. "I just lost my job," she said, her voice cracking. "I just lost everything."

I frowned. "I'm s-sorry," I said, trying hard not to sound drunk, though I was without a doubt hammered. Why did I do that? Just for once, I wanted to be aware of what was going on.

"That makes two of us," I added. "Tried physics, dropped out of college. Turns out the world can, can't be saved so . . . so what's the point?" There I went, making it about me. I realized that, but to my surprise, my comment made the girl smile, so I continued. "Fuck whoever hurt you. I'm going to, I'll make sure they pay one day. You deserve to be happy, i-if only for a few hours."

The girl smiled and finally looked up at me. When she did, her smile vanished and her eyes widened.

Her expression surprised me, and I pulled back from my position resting against the counter and sloshed some of my beer on my shirt. "Dammit! I mean, I'm . . . I'm sorry. I did, didn't mean to offend you."

She shook her head. "I can't believe it." She shut her eyes tight, then opened them again and shook her head once more. "Do you recognize me?"

"No," I mumbled. "I would, wouldn't forget your face."

She didn't smile that time, just stared at me. "I've seen you before . . . in a dream. It was—no, it's stupid. Maybe I'm just losing my mind. It's been a long day."

I shrugged. "Maybe I just look like the guy. I have a pretty average face."

She shook her head again. "No, no. You don't."

I smirked and told her to tell me about the dream. I wished at the time that she really had dreamt of me, though she was so far out of my league it was laughable.

"I can't remember it all," she said, her brows drawn together in concentration. "I just know I was so scared. I kept losing you—I mean, whoever it was—and, eventually, I couldn't find them. I was completely alone, and everything was dark and hot—" she broke off. "It's stupid, really." She laughed lightly but still looked disturbed. "I'm just upset from earlier, that's all. But let's drink."

I nodded, not making any sense of what she told me. "Now that is something I can understand."

"To new friends," she said, lifting her glass of beer.

"To old friends," I corrected her, and we both laughed.

After we took a drink, she ran her fingers through her long, dark brown hair and chuckled. "I like you, stranger. What's your name?"

I held out my hand to shake hers. "I'm Adam."

Once again, her smile disappeared. "Excuse me?"

"It's Adam. M-my name is—" But before I could finish, she was out of her seat and walking hurriedly toward the exit.

The last thing I'd remembered was taking the rest of the shot I'd ordered and making a pact with myself to never talk to another woman in my entire life. Then I'd gotten so drunk, I'd forgotten I'd ever met a beautiful girl who'd dreamt of me once.

I shook my head, bringing myself back to reality, and looked at Eve. She'd been watching me for far longer than I realized. Who was she, and why had she come looking for me again? Why had she freaked out, and what did the dream mean?

The man's voice on the Monitor was riddled with anxious anticipation. "Full power has been restored to the Capital and other cities around the Regime, except for major hazard zones including Denver and Cincinnati, which remain under quarantine. Access has been blocked into Cincinnati. People searching for family members are urged to stay in their respective regions until the critical areas have been assessed and rescue teams have been deployed. We've been getting requests about the length of the quarantine, and we remain uncertain. The Heads of State are still making decisions based on information that came in from the outposts regarding your safety and that of those you love. We are also receiving inquiries about the outage of the Screens around the Regime. Until we know the full extent of the damage to energy and electrical systems, the Screens will remain dark. Please send a signal to receive real-time footage through your Monitors from drones stationed around the Regime to get a look at the catastrophe brought about by these natural disasters."

My fists clenched. Was this nothing but a show to them? I clicked off the Monitor still hidden in the collar of the uniform and refocused on Eve. What was I going to say to her? Would I tell her that I remembered seeing her at the bar?

I watched her as she continued to look out the window of the machine with her big brown eyes. How long had she been watching me? That day at the bar was a little over a year ago. Her eyes focused on my reflection in the window as I looked at her. She grinned, and despite what I'd remembered— despite that I continued to be more and more confused about her motives—her smile made me feel better, and for a moment, it didn't feel like we were heading toward our probable deaths. For a moment, I forgot she was the girl who ran away from me. But nothing so simple, so sweet, seemed to last long. She *had* been watching me based on something she saw in a dream. Something tragic happened to her that day. Had I somehow caused it? She didn't seem like a vengeful person, but people could seem like a lot of things. She had ulterior motives; I just didn't know what they were yet. That was going to change.

I reached out and took her hand with my gloved one, and her fingers stopped tapping nervously as I did, then I laced my fingers through hers. If she started to trust me, maybe she'd tell me who she was and what she wanted. Maybe she'd give me the truth.

Her fingers tightened around mine, and I noticed Aimee glaring at me out of the corner of my eye. Was suspicion hidden in her desire to come with us?

Stop it, Adam. There's no use coming up with conspiracy theories.

"Look!" Aimee gasped and pointed out her window. "I've never been this far north before. I've always wanted to see Lake Michigan."

Miles laughed half-heartedly. "Too bad the reason you're finally here is because the world is ending."

Avery elbowed him in the side. "We decided to be optimistic, remember?"

"Just being realistic," Miles said.

"The view from up here is beautiful. Terrifying, but beautiful," Eve murmured. Her hand was still intertwined with mine, and I leaned over her shoulder to get a better look out the window. There were tracks, shut down at the time, running the length of the highway the autonome was driving on, several hundred feet to the right. The machine was gliding across the road, and we were the only ones in sight. We'd only passed a handful of other emergency autonomes, but no one ever stopped to question us.

We were alone at this point, and the machine had slowed down. The highway, though intended for official personnel-use only, was scenic and beautifully constructed. It was built of a lightweight, durable material whose see-through substance reminded me the Dome, but unlike the "protective" sphere around the Regime, this highway was made of real materials, not synthesized digitally.

Below us, the choppy water of Lake Michigan, the last remaining great lake in the Regime, was ink black. The silver light of the moon reflected off the large waves, and I barely noticed the trash floating in the black liquid, waiting to reach the shore.

"How about you, Hanson? Ever been out this way on

business?" Cal asked.

"No," I replied honestly. "Born and raised in Vegas and have been there since. Never had an assignment outside the city."

"Same here," Miles said. There was a sense of longing in his tone. "I wish my husband could've been here to see this."

Cal patted his shoulder, and the men went silent again. I focused on the GPS still visible on the machine's dashboard. We were almost across the lake, heading for Detroit, which lay on the Border like Las Vegas. It was our entry point back into the Dome. From there, Cincinnati was only a couple hours south.

Knowing we still had time, I focused my attention back on the water below. It reminded me of the painting I'd seen in middle school: *The Last Judgement.* Underneath the central skeletal figure in it that was thought to represent Death were mangled bodies being consumed by hideous creatures that could only be produced in nightmares. You could clearly see these figures with their twisted, disfigured expressions and their corpses forever being torn apart, though they were surrounded by darkness. There was another painting that stuck with me since those years by an artist called Rogier van der Weyden. In this similar painting, humans were cast into a darkness—an abyss—filled with fire. There was no fire on Lake Michigan, but its ink-black waters resembled those seen in the paintings. I pictured people being consumed by its darkness and the unknown creatures beneath the choppy water. This seemed so far away from reality. At least, that was what I used to believe.

I wished I could tell Eve about it. My plan to get her to trust me and explain who she was and what she wanted was being diminished by my not being able to talk to her in front of these men who didn't know we were involved in the outbreak at the Border or that Eve had killed a security agent. Though we'd made it out of being taken back to Vegas, I still felt uneasy. My heartbeat wouldn't slow down, no matter how hard I tried to calm myself. There was nothing calming about our situation, murder aside. I almost longed to be back at the bar, but I'd taken the easy way out for too long.

"There's a smaller city outside Cincinnati," Cal began as we crossed over the lake, leaving behind the invisible highway and my thoughts of *The Last Judgement.* "Dayton. We could stop there to regroup, and Aimee could get a sense of the safety level before we go headfirst into the Red Zone." Aimee had been the one trying to figure out where was the best place to stop based on her knowledge of the seismic activity around the area.

"That works for me," she said. "It's close enough that I can get a strong seismic signal but far enough away that we should be safe—relatively, at least—if plate activity starts to pick up again." She was holding her electronic tablet in her hands; red rings expanded and contracted in points surrounding the major fault line running through Cincinnati, which meant it was still active.

"It's stable, for now," she said when she noticed I was watching the screen.

"Doesn't look exactly stable," I replied grimly.

"Well, we're getting closer to the epicenter along the Cincinnati Arch Fault, but we're not experiencing any tremors, which is a good sign for the time being. Typically regions within 30 miles of an earthquake's epicenter still experience the full effects of the fault rupture. We should be far enough away that we don't while we're in Dayton, but after that . . . We just have to keep monitoring the activity and make sure it's safe for us to try and go into Cincinnati for search and rescue. Then it's just a matter of getting people as far away from the hazard zones as possible."

I took an uneasy breath. I knew enough to know that even with Aimee monitoring the activity, it would be impossible to know when an earthquake would occur or how bad it would be. I watched her as her eyes scanned the screen rapidly.

"The Cincinnati Arch Fault Zone didn't use to be active and didn't exist in the recent past. A few weeks before the major earthquake in Cincinnati, I recorded a magnitude 2 tremor along the fault closer to Lexington but didn't think it was cause for any alarm. The Regime experiences hundreds of thousands of earthquakes a year, but their effects are generally unnoticeable."

She paused and sighed audibly. "Then it happened again along the same fault. A magnitude 6, but it was deep below the surface, so it was only an intensity 7. It was the first sign of the fault slipping and shifting to create a fissure. The ground ejected some mud, but again, it wasn't reported through the Monitors and Screens because it wasn't seen as serious. I knew there was activity, but nothing would have led me to believe that an earthquake with intensity 11 would strike, and right in the middle of the city. It only covered around 4 miles through downtown, but the amount of damage at that intensity was *horrifying*."

We all listened intently as she told us the details of the aftermath of the Cincinnati earthquake, some of which we'd seen on the Screens or through Monitors. *13,000 dead . . .* I remembered the media coverage of the catastrophe the day it happened and how many people didn't seem to care.

Broad, deep fissures appeared that day, underground water and gas pipes broke, people were crushed by falling buildings, and the major Tramway connected to the communications building in the city center collapsed. Not to mention the massive crack in Cincinnati, the recurring earthquakes, and the landslides that took place in the areas surrounding the city in the days following the quake, as well as the fires from the gas leaks.

"It wasn't your fault, Aimee," Eve said in a soothing voice. "You warned Defense and Security. You tried."

"I know." Aimee sighed. "That zone had been relatively inactive since it formed. We knew something was going on—dammit!" Her fists tightened around her tablet. "They should have listened to me."

"If we, if the people had been notified—" Cal started, but Miles cut him off.

"They probably wouldn't have listened."

"I sent a report to our main office in downtown Vegas, which I hoped would be forwarded to the Heads of State to take action, but nothing came of that," Aimee said dejectedly. "They didn't listen until the earthquake took so many lives. It was too late, and then it triggered the fault in the New Madrid Seismic Zone near St. Louis. It was less intense—a magnitude 6 with intensity 9—but there was still considerable damage to buildings, and the ground cracked visibly like it did in Cincinnati. That made them pay attention, once they were finally in danger themselves."

"We're the most technologically advanced we have ever been as a species, and yet we can't manage to share information to save each other's lives." Avery shook his head.

"It's our eternal paradigm," I said. "We see what we want to see."

"Which, for most people," Eve lamented, "has nothing to do with reality."

Aimee exhaled, a sad expression on her face. "I'm afraid the activity in the Cascadia Subduction Zone in the Northwest, as well as the continued movement in the New Madrid Zone, could cause the tension building up along the Cincinnati Arch to rupture. I'm afraid we could experience an intensity 12 quake."

The men in the front seat looked at one another worriedly. "Is that even possible?" Miles asked.

"Anything is possible," Aimee said gloomily. "After what we've seen, I know that for sure."

My grip on Eve's hand tightened. I didn't know exactly what an intensity 12 earthquake entailed, but from what we'd seen with those preceding it, I imagined the worst.

"Would you be able to see the waves?" Eve asked, her eyes wide with terror.

Aimee focused once more on her screen. I think focusing on her work made her feel like she had some control over her life and what was going to happen to us all. I saw there were tears in her eyes. It was terrifying to think about what was most likely inevitable.

"We'd be thrown into the air, even in a vehicle like this built for stabilization to avoid fatal accidents. Outside the machine, we wouldn't be able to balance ourselves on the ground or focus on anything. And yes, we'd be able to see the waves."

"Waves?" Cal gaped.

"Seismic waves," Aimee clarified. "They're waves of energy that travel through the Earth after a quake. At that intensity, the seismic energy would create waves like those seen in water but on the ground."

My heart began to beat faster again, and I felt my blood pressure rising. I looked at her screen; nothing had changed, yet I was more terrified than I'd ever been in my entire life. The probability we'd die was high.

"How would that compare to San Andreas?" Miles asked.

I wasn't born when it happened, but everyone from that generation on remembered. An aggravated fault had caused part of the western-most section of the Regime to break off along the coast.

"It was a magnitude 9, wasn't it?" Cal put in.

Aimee nodded. "But it was different from what's happening now. Two major tectonic plates—the Pacific and North American—were rubbing against one another along the San Andreas Fault, and major quakes had been going on for a long time in that region. That, along with the rising sea levels and the sinking earth, finally caused that section to descend into the ocean. It was gradual. What happened there made sense, but now . . ."

CHAPTER 12

We arrived in the small city of Dayton around 4:30 in the morning. There were distant sirens, but we were far enough away from downtown that the blaring lights and crowds of people evacuating were nowhere to be seen. I gazed up at the row of street lights lining the suburban road that were still brightly lit, thanks to a combination of solar and wind energy. Small moths and June beetles bounced off their lights. Did they realize what was happening to us? I watched a spider weave a web under an overhanging light, and it wasn't long before several insects were ensnared, wriggling around to get free. I cringed as the arachnid encased one of the beetles. The bug had so easily fallen into the spider's trap. Had we fallen into Nature's? Humans had neglected the world we'd evolved on for our own selfish needs for so long. Was this our punishment?

I looked down the street at the never-ending rows of houses. Under normal circumstances, there would still be occasional traffic from public transportation—it would be private automatic transport if we were in a high-class area—and we might even see some people, though my guess was we wouldn't come across anyone directly. They'd exit the bus and go straight into their homes, if they even left their houses at all. No one necessarily had to leave. A person could contact anyone they wanted, see anything they desired, and order food whenever they needed it with their Monitor. But people had already evacuated this area and many others surrounding the fault zones. Aimee had told us that people were being ordered to go to some of the more northern cities in the Regime, including Des Moines, Omaha, Sioux Falls, and Bismarck. Some used public transport and others went on foot after they received the signal. If anyone was left in this suburb, we didn't see them.

We stood around Aimee in a patch of grass. The earthquake in Cincinnati was the farthest north of those taking place along the Arch Fault. There wasn't any noticeable damage in this area. Yet, at least.

Aimee's electronic tablet rested on a synthesized platform before her, having had its screen expand as well. It was measuring seismic activity below the Earth's surface, though I was clueless to how it worked. Eve said something about subtle vibrations and energy waves, which made sense, but I wasn't paying attention.

After a few minutes of silence, Eve pulled me to the side. The three agents were walking up and down the street, knocking on doors and searching for people that hadn't left, so we were alone. Finally.

"Do you trust her?" I asked, inclining my head toward Aimee. They'd known one another, and Aimee seemed protective of Eve—she'd been willing to attack me at the outpost, not knowing that I wasn't a real agent—but Aimee still had a Monitor, just like the men, though she knew the truth and they didn't.

"With my life," Eve said with a nod. "We started off working together at the outpost when my department began assigning scientists to work more closely alongside the engineers, but she became my best friend." She frowned. "I know it probably didn't seem like it. I'm sorry you had to see us fight; that was my fault. I shouldn't have accused her of hiding from what's happening. I know she cares about her job, and I'm sure she's been under a lot of stress. I don't know. I just get so angry when I see those Screens. They're like the

Monitors. What they can do is incredible and sometimes breathtaking, but they're also controlling and slowly killing people . . ."

She watched Aimee typing away on her tablet. "Some part of me still wishes I was an engineer. It wasn't my choice to leave, and I loved what I did, but the other part of me is happy I left and happy I don't have a Monitor anymore. I just feel guilty about leaving Aimee. She helped me through a lot, and then I left without warning. I should've contacted her before now, but I felt like I had to get as far away from anything that reminded me of what happened as I could. I couldn't go on pretending everything was okay and nothing had changed. Maybe that's childish of me, but I had to leave that life behind."

I understood what she meant. I'd tried running away from my past for so long. I'd been angry when she'd said I'd wanted a fresh start, but she'd been right. It wasn't the only reason I'd left the Dome, but it was definitely one of them.

"What happened to you?" I asked after a moment, thinking about her running out of the bar when I'd told her my name. She'd told me she'd lost her job that night. I had a feeling it wasn't her fault, and I wanted answers. I couldn't piece together what had happened that day, why she'd come looking for me again, and why she'd targeted me to help her break through the Border. She would've been able to do it on her own, without a doubt.

"I was taken advantage of," she said, her eyes falling to the ground. I'd never seen her look so sad. It was just like the day at the bar. "To put it lightly, anyway. When you and I arrived at the outpost and Aimee threatened you, well, I guess you could say that was PTSD."

"A security agent hurt you?"

"Raped." She said the word in a hushed voice, and I almost didn't hear her, but I did. My heart sank, and my stomach turned sickeningly. It wasn't her "sister." It was her. This girl who had to live as someone else had been hurt far worse than I ever imagined.

"Eve, I'm so sorry."

"Don't be. I've spent too long feeling sorry for myself, wondering what I did to deserve what happened. The truth of the matter is that the agent could have done it to anyone. It just so happened to be me that time."

I wanted to claw the helmet off, light the uniform on fire, and make sure there was nothing left of it. I felt dirty. How could she stand to look at me wearing it?

They're not all like that, don't forget. A couple of security agents had helped me when I was younger. They taught me how to hide myself, how to pretend I was normal, but this was something I could not forgive. How could anyone hurt her and get pleasure from it? I could tear my eyes out picturing what happened.

"I'm sorry I lied. I didn't do it to deceive you specifically; it's just easier for me to lie and remove myself from what I went through. I did have a sister, though. That part is true. She died when she was young." Eve blinked back tears and shook her head. "I lost my job and had to completely change my identity because of what the agent did to me. Because *he* reported *me*. I was accused of committing his crime. I would've gone to jail, or worse. I could've tried to fight it, but there was no hope. Agents are respected, not some random data engineer who had a history of stealing when she was younger. I'd tried to make myself better. I'd gone to college, got a high-security job, and for what?"

"Eve," I started, but what could I say? What could possibly make any of that better?

She smiled weakly and straightened up. "I'm okay. Let's not talk about the past anymore. We need to focus on what's happening now."

That was important, but so were her feelings. She shouldn't have to hide them, and she was still hurting; that was obvious. "Okay, but if you need to talk, I'm here. I can't imagine what it was like going through what you did and having to change your entire life because of it, but I do know what it's like to lose someone, and I understand having to hide who you are. I've been doing it my entire life."

She smiled again. "Thank you."

I knew she was upset, and I didn't want to push her, but I also didn't know how long we had to talk alone. I couldn't go on without knowing why she'd come looking for me. I had to tell her I remembered meeting her at the bar.

"There's something else," I started, growing more nervous at how she'd react or what she'd say. I didn't know what to expect. Why didn't she tell me she'd seen me before?

"What? Tell me."

"I know."

She looked at me quizzically.

"I mean, I remember seeing you at the Back Door way before I worked there."

Her eyes widened in realization. "How?"

"The tapping," I said, pointing to her fingers. "I remembered you tapping your fingers on the bar counter. You were so sad." My body deflated at the memory. "Then you told me you had seen me before. Eve"—I held my hand up for her to stop when she started to say something—"I don't care if you've been watching me, though I feel sorry for you if you have. My life isn't exactly eventful. All I want to know is why. Why did you run?"

She bore her eyes into the ground. "Your life isn't boring, first off. You help people in need, and you're kind. I've seen you at the shelters downtown. I've seen you talk to people at the bar and help them find meaning in their lives when they feel like there's nothing left. You're a good person."

She continued when I didn't say anything, "I started having vivid night terrors and experiencing sleep paralysis a few months before I became Ara. I would be asleep but would think I was awake and couldn't move. It was terrifying. I don't know exactly how to explain it, but these terrors were mixed with nightmares where I would be walking through the woods. Then, I would end up in this wide-open place—a field. It was beautiful, all grass and wildflowers, but it didn't last. I would see a man. He was, he looked . . ."

Her face screwed up in confusion. "He looked just like you. He was . . . handsome, like you. I wanted to be near him, but when I started walking toward him, the same feeling I had during sleep paralysis would come back. My muscles would seize up, and I would be frozen. Then this crack would start forming in the ground, like the fault, and I would be so afraid you were going to fall in. I never saw if you did. I would wake up just in time, screaming your name. *Adam.* And then, out of nowhere, I found you in a bar when my world was falling apart. I never met you. I was more terrified than when the security agent held me down, but for an entirely different reason. You were real. Your name, everything, I mean, it all added up. I ran because I didn't know what else to do. But I couldn't stay away. The dreams continued, all variations of the same one, and I couldn't stop thinking about you. I started following you the week after that day at the bar and was there one night a couple weeks ago when you fell asleep. I was in a booth, pretending to watch the Screen. Linda let you sleep, and we talked for a while. Then I heard someone scream. It was you—"

Whatever else she said, I didn't hear it. Her dream was the same as mine. It was so vivid. I was sitting in the grass next to the cat on a beautiful day, the same day Eve described, and the sun was shining. A girl stood under a tree. It was Eve. I understood now why I'd dreamt of her before I'd seen her at the station: because I'd met her at the Back Door. The dreams started right around that time, so it made sense, but she'd been having them for far longer, and she'd dreamt of the fault. How was that possible?

"Adam?" Eve grabbed my shoulders and shook me. Down the road, I heard Miles calling, "Anyone there?"

She looked at me expectantly. "Please tell me there's something you know that I don't. I've been trying to figure out how I dreamt of you. I'd never seen you before; I know that for a fact. Or, I thought I did, but that's the only thing that makes sense, right? You have to know something."

I focused on her face, trying to remember something about

her, anything that would tell me I'd known her before. That a stranger hadn't dreamt of me. But I couldn't. The first time I'd seen her was at the Back Door.

"Adam!" She shook me again, harder. She was growing hysterical. "Do you know something I don't?" Her big brown eyes were fixed on me, and she looked on the verge of tears. "I just want to understand."

"No," I muttered, feeling completely lost. "No, I don't. I thought you did." Everything was supposed to fall into place once she explained what she knew, but we were both in the dark.

Her face fell instantly. "When I followed you, when I watched you, I hoped you would do something, say something that would help me understand why I kept seeing your face in my dreams, and I brought you with me not only because I knew you'd want to help people, but also because I couldn't stand leaving you behind in Vegas without knowing why—why was I led to you? And how . . . how did I see the fault before it happened?" She seemed to ask herself the question more than me.

"It doesn't make sense," she added. "I don't blame you if you think I'm some psychopathic stalker, dragging you along with me, making you commit crimes and kissing you . . . I don't know how to explain it, but I feel like I know you. I felt that way even before I started watching you. That's why I told Aimee we'd known each other for a long time." She shook her head. "That was what I kept telling myself to try to make sense of it anyways. I know I promised back at the station that I'd explain everything, but the only thing I know is the dream."

She stared at her feet. "Once the earthquake struck and I saw the crack in Cincinnati—when it seemed like the dream was getting more and more real—I knew I couldn't hide from it, or from you, anymore." She let out a heavy sigh. "I thought I had this grand plan of breaking out of the Dome, getting to Cincinnati, and trying to save people. I thought by doing that, I don't know, that I could somehow stop the dream from becoming reality—that I could rewrite it in some way—and I knew I couldn't do it without you."

I took a deep breath, trying to wrap my mind around it. She was right; it didn't make sense. There had to be an explanation. We just didn't know it yet. "All I know is that you didn't make me do anything," I said. "I came with you because I wanted a change, and I wanted it with you. When you kissed me, I wanted that. I keep wanting that. I barely know you, yet I feel so drawn to you. And these dreams . . . I started having the same one you described about a year ago, except there wasn't a fault—I didn't dream of that until Cincinnati. I didn't understand how I'd seen you in my dreams, though, but it makes sense now that I remember meeting you at the bar. But I don't understand how you had them before that or how it's even possible for us to be experiencing almost the exact same thing."

"Me neither." She cursed under her breath and wiped a tear from her eye. "I'm tired of being scared and confused and"—she glanced in the direction of Aimee's tablet—"I don't want to die."

I lifted her chin to where her face met my own. "We'll be okay. We'll figure this out." I didn't entirely believe what I said, but it felt good to say. I just hoped we *would* figure it out; there had to be an explanation.

Her eyes searched for mine, but she couldn't see me under the helmet. I moved my hands to take it off, but she stopped me. "Don't. We don't know if it's safe."

Now that I knew more about her and that she hadn't led me here for some malicious reason, I felt closer to her. I looked at her lips, thinking about our moment in the desert. "Eve—"

"Avery, get over here!" Cal, Avery, and Miles had made their way back up the opposite side of the street. I didn't see them, but their shadows were just visible from behind the house across from us as a yard light shown down on them.

"Miles, it's a girl!"

Eve pulled away from me as a shrill screech pierced the air. It was a girl's voice. "No! Leave me alone!"

Eve glanced at me, then started running toward the back

of the house, and I followed quickly.

"Let me go!" the girl yelled, her voice echoing in the silence.

"We're not here to hurt you," Cal said.

"We're here to save you," Miles assured her, but she didn't listen as she thrashed around in Avery's arms in the back yard of a house identical to all the others on the street.

"Stop!" Eve demanded. "You're scaring her!"

The girl stopped yelling once she saw Eve. Tears streaked her face, and she appeared terrified. Her clothes were fairly clean, but her jeans had mud stains on the knees and crumpled leaves stuck out of her wild black hair. Her grey-blue eyes moved between Eve and me, and her lower lip quivered. "Please don't kill me."

"We're not going to harm you in any way," Eve said as she knelt next to the girl. She had light brown skin, and freckles covered her entire face, like a thousand tiny stars. She couldn't be more than 12.

I held out my gloved hand to her. "You're safe." I wanted to make her feel better, but it was a lie. None of us were truly safe.

A tear ran down the girl's face. "My brother used to tell me never to trust security agents."

"It's alright," Eve said calmly. "He wants to help you. We all do. My name is Ara. This is Hanson, Miles, Avery, and Cal. What's your name?"

The girl didn't say anything, just kept looking at her reflection in my helmet. "What's your name?" I asked her again.

All of a sudden, she thrust her elbow back into Avery's side and tore out of his arms. Before he could stop her, she was crashing into me, throwing her arms around me in a hug. Her whole body shook from sobbing, and all she managed to say was, "My name is Emi."

Without the Dome over us, it would probably be too hot to be outside, but here we sat in the midmorning sun. Eve had hacked into an alarm system on one of the houses, and Avery found food inside to cook for us all. I fell asleep for a few hours, but before I knew it, it was my turn to watch over the group. Eve kept her eyes glued on Aimee's device while she rested, and Emi had finally drifted into sleep, her head lying in my lap. I smiled, though no one saw my face. I frowned when I thought of that. The men were asleep. Even if they weren't, what did it matter if they saw my face? Why was I hiding? If Defense and Security managed to figure out Eve and I had caused the outbreak at the Border, they'd have pictures of both of us plastered across the media, and Eve hadn't been hiding under a helmet. If the men we were with figured out she was involved, it wouldn't be long before they figured out I was too, with or without the helmet. There was a very slight chance they wouldn't discover the truth, and if they did, I'd never keep pretending to be an agent and let her take the fall for it alone.

I took the glossy black helmet off without another thought and laid it down beside me in the grass. I didn't want to hide anymore. If the world went to shit and these were my last days, I wanted to see with my eyes, not through a mask.

Emi mumbled in her sleep, though I only understood a fraction of what she said. She was speaking a foreign language. French, from what I gathered. There weren't many people in the Regime left that spoke anything but English. Like many things of our distant past, language was lost and only remembered by people who were considered less than everyone else: the Untouchables.

When I was about ten years old, going between orphanages, I met a boy who was part of their group. He was the one who taught me how to write, and he even taught me some phrases in Russian and French, though I could barely remember them. I envied the life Aaron led, and I told him that right up until the day he disappeared.

Emi rolled over on her side, her head falling from my lap to the soft grass. She reminded me of the little girl I saw on the Screen, but Emi was alive. I was going to try and save her. I hoped to, anyway.

Before she'd fallen asleep, she'd told me about her home. She'd lived a couple miles east of Dayton on a large, run-down farm with her older sister who'd raised her. They were part of a larger community of Untouchables living in the country. She told me she'd been so excited because she found out her sister was pregnant and she was going to be an aunt. She was going to teach the baby how to fish, how to grow all her favorite fruits and vegetables (blackberries and butternut squash, as she'd pointed out enthusiastically), how to raise chickens and collect eggs, and, most importantly, how to see the world differently. That was before she started to sob again and revealed that her brother had been a security agent. He'd died in a building collapse during the major Cincinnati earthquake. She told me I reminded her of him and that he'd told her about the corruption within Defense and Security. She thought his death wasn't an accident. I told her that not all security agents were bad, but all she said was that she believed I wasn't. I hoped I could prove that to her.

"You would've loved it on the farm," she'd said in between tears. "And my sister, you would've liked her. Everyone did. She's a wonderful painter. I wish I still had one of her sketches of us . . ."

"I'm so sorry, Emi," I'd said as she sniffled.

"I wish I was as strong as your friend," she said, pointing at Eve, who stood next to Aimee. "They're both so smart, but Ara seems fearless."

"She's been through a lot," I told Emi. "Just like you."

Emi wiped her nose with her sweater. "I don't want to be out here alone anymore."

"You don't have to be. We're here with you. We won't leave."

"I don't know where my sister is," she'd said after a while, holding tightly to my hand. I think she was afraid that if she let go, she'd lose her brother all over again. "There were some people in our group who were convinced this is the end of the world. They wanted us to commit suicide, but that wasn't their choice. They were always a little radical, but that was crazy. Kill ourselves? We didn't pay much attention to them until last weekend. They decided we should all die. My sister told me to run, and that's what I did."

I wanted to scream. I wanted to throw things and hurt the people that did that to her, but then Emi looked at me. Her blue-grey eyes were wide—there were puffy bags under them from exhaustion—and her face was red and blotchy from crying. All I wanted was to be able to tell her everything would be okay. I couldn't do that, but she made me realize there was nothing more important than making sure she felt like life was worth living again.

"Why did they do that?" I asked, sickened at the thought of Emi waking up to these people standing over her, murder in their expressions.

She took a sharp breath, trying to stop herself from crying, and looked up at the sky. "They said it was for Him."

My mouth fell open in an instant, and the words the old woman had uttered at the tracks came flooding back to me. *"He's watching . . ."* Suddenly, things were beginning to click. The old woman had killed herself because she couldn't stand to live in a world so self-centered it didn't care that people were dying, or so I thought. Maybe that wasn't the exact reason. What if she threw herself onto the tracks because, like the people Emi spoke of, she thought the world was ending, and she thought "He" wanted her to die?

"Emi, who were they doing it for? The people at the farm? Who is 'He'?"

She cocked her head to the side and looked at me questioningly. "You don't know?"

"No. Please tell me."

"I thought they were our friends." She shook her head in disappointment and wiped away the tears she'd been trying to stop. "They didn't do it because they hated us. They did it because they loved us and thought it was the right thing to do and that we'd be saved." More tears fell down her face, and I held her hand for comfort. "Some people believe in Him;

some people believe in other versions of Him. I never agreed with what the others at the farm said, but I listened."

I nodded for her to continue and shot a quick glance at Eve. She was watching us intently, though I didn't think she heard what Emi said because she was smiling. I motioned for her to join us, and as soon as she sat down, Emi told us about "Him."

Emi did and said things that made her seem like a little girl, but she was also extremely intelligent and would say things that were more mature than what some adults I'd come across in my life did. She was caught between being young and innocent and having experienced things far beyond her years.

She said that "He" was thought by some to be a being more powerful and beneficent than any other form of intelligent life that had ever lived. Some people thought he was the first intelligent life and that all others came from Him. She told us He wasn't really a man; that was just something people used to define the being. She also talked about a serene place called Heaven and a horrific place called Hell that was filled with fire. Good people went to Heaven; bad people to Hell. The people at her farm that had wanted everyone to commit suicide thought that was the brave thing to do and that they'd meet "Him" in Heaven.

Then she told us something that made my heart skip a beat and my pulse begin to race. She said the radicals at her farm and others around the Regime called what was happening Judgement Day.

"They believe it's punishment for our sins, but why should my brother have been punished? He was a good person. And my sister? Her baby? Why would this being let them be taken away from me if they had the power to stop it?"

Emi had a point. The beliefs she described seemed so far removed from reality, but apparently, there were people that put faith in them, though those individuals were far removed from the society the Regime had built. I'd never heard anyone speak about anything to do with religion outside of that one day in middle school until the old woman . . . But she hadn't been an Untouchable; she'd had a Monitor. The only explanation was that she must have been an Untouchable at one point in her life, and though her speech had been distorted, she'd spoken about the exact things Emi did. The old woman was probably separated from her group as a child, allowing the government to take her in as an orphan and force her to undergo the Monitor implantation.

I started to picture her throwing herself onto the tracks, and I quickly shook away my thoughts of her and refocused on what Emi was talking about. The people in her group who'd believed in "Him" and had wanted to kill everyone believed what was happening to our world was punishment for what she called "sins," which she later said could be thought of as the things we'd done wrong to each other and the world, and included being hateful, greedy, lustful, and gluttonous.

I didn't fully understand what she meant, and I couldn't understand how that would lead anyone to want to kill themselves or others. I could grasp that people would be angry about what we'd done to the Earth, but being angry was different than thinking everyone deserved to die for what generations upon generations had done before us, and even though some of those things were still happening, that didn't mean everyone was a part of them. That didn't mean everyone deserved to die.

Why would anyone believe this being would want that or had caused any of what was going on? It seemed like the radicals in Emi's group were grasping for explanations for things that they didn't fully understand, or things that terrified them, or maybe they really thought sacrificing themselves would serve some higher purpose. She'd said they'd thought it would bring them closer to salvation and to Him.

It was so foreign from anything I'd ever heard about. There *were* explanations for most things, and for others, I accepted the fact that humans could never fully understand our world and others, or even ourselves for that matter. But who was I to say that the opinion of the people in Emi's group was wrong? Making the choice to die yourself was one thing, but I would never be able to wrap my head around anyone wanting to kill other people for any reason besides self-defense. Life was absolute shit at times, but it was also beautiful.

"It can't be true," Eve said when Emi finished, her fists clenched angrily. "Who could let this happen to innocent people?"

Emi frowned. "I don't know. I didn't understand what they were talking about. My sister and I don't believe in Him. There were others at the farm that did, but they weren't like the ones that wanted us to die. I think believing gave them joy, but they weren't radical. They didn't think this is Judgement Day or that all of the bad stuff that's been happening is punishment for our sins."

"Do you know anything else?" I asked her quickly, but she shook her head.

"I just know that not all religion is bad." She paused for a minute, thinking. "There was a radio station I heard someone talking about the day before—" Her voice broke. "Before the others tried to hurt us." Tears started to form in the corners of her eyes again, and Eve wrapped her arms around her.

Emi continued, her voice muffled as she half buried her face in Eve's shirt, "They said a group of Untouchables outside Cincinnati hijacked a station's signal. I think"—she took in a deep breath, trying to calm herself—"it has something to do with people debating what's going on. I don't know if it has to do with religion or if it's actually real."

Eve looked at me with raised eyebrows.

"Do you think they could actually be using a broadcast signal?" I asked.

"With everything that's going on, people aren't paying as much attention as they usually do. So, yes, I think they could."

Without hesitation, I dug the Monitor out of my pocket. Emi pulled away from Eve and looked at me, her mouth open in surprise, but didn't say anything; maybe she'd feel better knowing she wasn't the only one without a Monitor.

"Ad—" Eve stopped herself. "Hanson. Put that away.

What are you thinking?" She glanced nervously behind her at the agents.

"Shhh," I whispered and tucked it under my helmet after I shoved the earpiece in, then started scanning the stations. I wasn't going to get caught; the three agents were already fast asleep.

I'd spent over twenty minutes searching for the right broadcast signal with no luck until Eve had finally come back over and demanded I take it out. I'd humored her, but whether it proved useless or not, I would keep searching.

I pulled myself from my thoughts and looked down at Emi, still asleep in the grass. My eyes flickered over to Eve. She was still watching Aimee's device. I hadn't been able to find the station Emi had told us about before, but I was still determined. I pulled my Monitor from my pocket and put in the earpiece again.

I watched Emi's chest rise and fall as I scanned the channels. Like Eve, I hadn't known Emi long, but I felt like I had to protect her. I didn't want her to die like the little girl I'd seen on the Screen, and I reminded her of her brother. I could never take his place, but I'd try as hard as I could to make sure she found some joy in life. Too many bad things had happened to her. She was intelligent and sometimes said things that made her seem mature beyond her years, but she was still a little girl. She loved life and had lost her sister because some psychopaths decided everyone in their group should die. How could anyone justify that?

I couldn't accept that the people who'd tried to hurt Emi had wanted to sacrifice themselves and their group for some higher power. Then there were the places she'd described, Heaven and Hell. How could anyone believe in that? But they did, and so did the old woman at the tracks. The otherworldly scenes of death and suffering that had stuck with me since middle school seemed like they weren't just the nightmarish visions of artists after all.

I exhaled slowly. I'd been through over a hundred stations and still hadn't found the one Emi mentioned. My body was exhausted, but my brain felt like it was going a million miles a minute. I had to understand this, and searching for an answer seemed like a better use of my time than thinking about how our world had turned into the Hell Emi had described and how I'd most likely be killed as soon as the Officers got ahold of us. I didn't want to believe it, but it seemed like it was only a matter of time.

Stop it. Focus on Emi and Eve. But I felt like my time with them was ticking away faster and faster. It felt like the whole world was.

CHAPTER 13

Two days had passed, and nothing had changed the way I expected it to.

One minute, Aimee was screaming, telling us to take shelter because she was receiving strong seismic signals on her device from the New Madrid Zone. The next, alerts went out across the Regime, the Capital was put on lockdown, and barriers were synthesized along the faults around the area within a couple hours radius of the major energy reading near St. Louis. That time, the Regime was prepared. Barriers were even synthesized along the Cincinnati Arch; no one was taking a chance. Engineers had also managed to divert the flooding that threatened to overwhelm the Pacific Northwest and eastern portions of the forcefield surrounding the Dome.

In the days leading up to that point, search and rescue teams had recovered hundreds of civilians, dead and alive, in the Red Zones. Those that willingly went were escorted from Cincinnati, Houston, Las Vegas, Denver, and the Capital to New Anchorage: the Regime's offshore holding across the Pacific. People who'd already been able to evacuate themselves or were fleeing the Red Zones to the more northern cities were told to shelter in place once they arrived there.

Eve had disabled the signal systems' ability to receive incoming waves in our Monitors and the autonome, allowing our group to go unnoticed in our empty suburb. Everything leading up to the energy surge had made it seem as though life might've been normal again one day.

The next thing I knew, we were sitting in the house, Eve and Emi clutching my arms, the three agents and Aimee gathered around us. Emi swore in French, and Eve held my hand so tightly, it went numb. We were far enough away from the New Madrid readings, but if an earthquake there triggered something along the Cincinnati Arch, we could die. The fault's energy was strong enough; it could very well trigger the Arch. Everyone in our group knew the risk, but we didn't acknowledge it out loud. Especially for Emi's sake. We just waited.

While we did, Avery told us about his husband. They dreamt of leaving the Dome and building a house somewhere in the desert together. They wanted a clean break from the politics and the societal pressure. He said he knew it would be impossible—that kind of freedom didn't exist—but he said they could still dream.

Cal talked about his training at the prestigious medical institution in St. Louis, the Freyman Institute, named after the brother and sister duo that developed the first cost-effective and sustainable long-term cancer cure. He dreamt of developing a preventative drug against AIDS to be injected directly into the womb before birth. It was rampant in inner-city communities in the Regime. Some things seemed impossible, but Cal said those were the ones worth fighting for the most.

Eve told us about her sister and how much she missed her. They'd grown up in a low-income area of Tucson, and their father had been an engineer for the Regime like Eve, though she'd made up a story about doing coding and software development for a company in Vegas to hide her identity from Cal, Avery, and Miles, and also explain how she knew to hack into different kinds of systems. The men seemed like good people, but they were still agents, meaning we'd never be safe around them.

Like Eve, her father had also lost his job, but for no other reason than he was making more money than the data engineers the company he'd worked for could hire right out of school. After that, he'd gotten so depressed that he'd started drinking and using drugs. Eve didn't talk about what happened to her sister but said that she'd basically acted as her guardian, stealing food and whatever else they needed. But Eve said that as long as they were together, they were happy, and that they'd dreamt of living on the Moon, somewhere they could see the real sky every night.

Emi talked about her sister, too, about her art and her love of literature, then confessed she wanted to be a writer when she grew up. She was fascinated by someone called Hemingway. I never heard the name, but then again, classical literature wasn't something that was promoted in the Regime. It was considered boring by most people.

Emi told us about Hemingway's adventures in a place called Paris. It made me smile to hear her talk so fondly of someone she never knew but cared about deeply. Most importantly, hearing other people talk about their dreams and speaking about her own took her mind off our situation.

She said the man, Hemingway, lost his mind after going through an intense medical treatment. He was in so much pain that he took his own life. I thought about people I'd met at the Back Door and what Eve said about giving people a reason to go on. It hurt to think about someone wanting to take their own life when they had the choice not to.

I told Emi not to think about death, but she said she wasn't afraid. She said dying made living even more beautiful. She continued surprising me with how intelligent and mature she was for her age.

I hoped we survived and I wasn't killed for impersonating a security agent. I wanted to help her find her sister and become the writer she wanted to be. She said she wished "Ara" and I could come live with them after this was over. Eve promised she would, and I couldn't say no to either one of them. My heart felt lighter when I saw them smile.

We sat in the living room of the house for over an hour. Then, just like that, the intense seismic waves deep below the surface disappeared. It was as if we'd imagined it all. Aimee pulled at her hair, her expression a mixture of anger and sadness. She was able to send signals to her colleagues in Las Vegas. She was the one who'd notified them of the energy readings on her device. I'd seen them with my own eyes; I knew it wasn't a mistake. But it went away without so much as a tremor. It didn't make sense . . . It wasn't possible.

"I like you better without the helmet, Hanson," Miles said as he sat next to me outside the house Eve had broken into. With her skill set, it made sense how easily she began to live as a criminal, as she referred to herself, after she was forced to change her identity. She could take whatever she wanted before anyone knew what happened, and she'd never been caught.

I ran my fingers through my hair. The wind against my face felt nice. "It feels good to be free of it," I said.

"I can imagine," Miles agreed. "The rescue division wanted us to adopt a similar uniform, helmet and all, but the director convinced the overseeing Head of State that it was too impersonal. People want to see a face, not some lifeless mirror resembling a robot, ironically enough."

"We try to convince ourselves it's for protection." Really, it was just another tool for surveillance.

Emi laughed uncontrollably as Aimee and Eve spun her around, dancing wildly in the back yard and drawing my attention away from my own worries.

"She's an incredible little girl," Miles said with a grin as he watched Emi. I was sure that was the first time I saw him smile. It faded quickly. "My husband and I wanted a daughter." He shook his head, trying to make the memory disappear, then looked at me, his blue eyes searching. "Do you love her? Ara, I mean."

"I—" I started, glancing at her. "What?" As far as the agents knew, we'd only met after the collapse of the Tramway

Eve had made up when they'd found us at the outpost. Had Defense and Security figured out what happened at the Border—that we'd caused the outbreak? Did the agents know we'd lied? I wanted to stand up immediately, get Emi and Eve, and start running as fast as we could, but I tried not to let myself lose control.

Breathe, Adam. You have to stay calm.

"I know you just met," Miles went on, and I relaxed slightly. "But it seems like you're both attracted to one another and, I don't know, you look at her the way I used to look at my husband."

No longer afraid we'd have to run for our lives, I leaned back and watched Eve. Her smooth, dark brown hair whipped in the wind as she spun around. She was incredible, but I barely knew her. "Can you love someone you barely know?"

Miles grinned again. "Love is rare, Hanson. Don't let her go."

I didn't plan on it. There was something between us that we didn't understand. Something had brought us together.

"Not that you're asking for my advice, but I wouldn't go back to Vegas, Hanson. Get some job that makes you happy. Marry that girl and give Emi a new home. Sure, you can make up some lie about not being able to contact the agency"—a real agent would get in a lot of trouble for going silent like Miles, Cal, and Avery thought I had—"but you'll never be happy, and they'll take Emi away from you. She's an Untouchable. She'll be thrown in an orphanage and forced to undergo the surgery to have a Monitor implanted."

I sighed. "I wish it was that easy."

"If you want something bad enough and know people willing to help, anything is possible. I shouldn't be saying this, but I have nothing left to lose. If I can make other people happy, I don't care what happens to me."

My eyebrows knit together in confusion. What was he trying to say? He didn't care what would happen to him? "Don't say that," I said. "You deserve happiness just as much as the rest of us."

Miles closed his eyes. I wondered what he saw when he did. "My happiness died with my husband. If I can help other people, maybe I'll find it again one day, but for now, this is what I want." He turned to look directly at me, and his voice suddenly became a whisper. "Listen, I know some people who can replace your identification chips and reconfigure your Monitors. It wouldn't be pleasant, but it would be a fresh start."

I stared at him, shocked. That was a major criminal offense; he couldn't be serious, but nothing in his expression told me he was joking.

I swallowed hard as I thought about what he said. Of course, it would mean he'd eventually figure out Eve and I did not have Monitors, but he didn't have to know that right now. If he was serious and he really had those connections, Eve, Emi, and I could be safe. "Thank you," I said simply. "If we make it out of this, I might take you up on that offer."

The Regime was conducting 24/7 surveillance of the fault zones and was on lockdown for the next 21 days. It would be 3 weeks until life was "normal" once more. 3 more weeks until Miles, Avery, and Cal returned to Las Vegas, making up some excuse about being taken hostage to cover up disappearing for that period of time. 21 days till Emi was taken away from us. As a minor, she'd be forced to go into an orphanage whether they found her sister or not. Untouchables weren't a part of our system; therefore, they weren't recognized as true citizens once they reached age 18, which meant her sister wouldn't be recognized as Emi's guardian. To the system, her sister didn't exist. Because of that and Emi's young age, she would be forced to have a Monitor. 21 days till I lost her, and most likely Eve. 21 days till I became Adam again, unless Miles could help us.

"Hanson!" Emi ran across the yard, her arms waving madly, and fell to the ground giggling beside Miles and me. "Come join us, both of you! Stop being so boring and have some fun!"

I laughed as she tugged on my arms to try and pull me up.

"Alright, alright. I'm getting up, I promise."

We sat around a fire Avery built in the back yard. Emi had taken a stick from a broken tree limb and fashioned it into a skewer. A hotdog from the owner's refrigerator was stuck haphazardly on the end.

"It's not as good as a marshmallow," she said with a grin, "but I'll take it." She shrugged and laughed again.

I watched the orange and yellow flames dance in front of her as she sat across the fire from me, the flames casting dark shadows like waves across her freckled face. No matter how hard I tried not to, I pictured the figures being thrown into the fire in Van der Weyden's painting. But I had to keep telling myself that Emi was alive and happy, despite everything. Hell wasn't real . . .

Eve stopped pretending she didn't want to be near me when everyone was watching. She was almost always by my or Emi's side. I swore I caught Cal smirking when she sat next to me and lay her head on my shoulder. Aimee just rolled her eyes.

Avery sat by Aimee quietly, his eyes rigidly fixed on the flames. He didn't seem to hear anything anyone said. Was he listening to his Monitor? When the others had fallen asleep the night before, I put the earpiece in and listened again for something about the Untouchables, but all I heard were plans of rebuilding and monuments erected in honor of fallen citizens. It was false hope, in my opinion, and nothing I'd wanted to hear.

I cleared my throat after a moment. "Thanks for the fire, Avery." Still, he didn't look away from the flames and didn't make a move to respond.

Cal's eyebrows drew together in concern. "Avery, you okay?"

No response.

Aimee nudged him lightly with her elbow. "Avery?"

His body jolted upright from its slumped position, and his head jerked back, startled. He blinked a few times, bringing himself back to reality, then his head shot around, looking between us all. His gaze finally landed on Eve and me. My heartbeat quickened as he spoke.

"I was just listening to a broadcast." He sounded unsure, or maybe it was suspicion. "There were images and everything."

"What?" Aimee blurted. "Did I miss something?" Her eyes quickly glazed over as she focused on the images in her Monitor, but Avery stopped her.

"No." He shook his head. "Nothing like that."

"What did you hear? Come on, man," Cal coaxed.

Avery's gaze never left Eve and me. "They have footage of the people who caused the breach at the Border in Vegas. The media is calling them terrorists."

Emi was so focused on what Avery said, her hotdog lit on fire. "*Putain*," she cursed under her breath.

"Why did you do it?" Avery asked, studying us.

Everyone's gaze turned toward us, their eyes locked on ours. I could feel myself starting to sweat. Was this it? Was Avery going to be the one to turn us in? Everyone looked confused. Everyone except Aimee.

"Tell them who you are," Avery said. His tone wasn't angry, but there was force behind his words.

I swallowed hard. *Just breathe, Adam, just breathe.*

But I could barely catch my breath, let alone think straight. "I have no idea what you're talking about." I tried to sound like I was telling the truth, but my voice was uneasy.

Avery narrowed his eyes. "There's no use lying."

He was right. If the media knew who caused the breach, then so would everyone with a Monitor. I felt like I was going to throw up. Everything came out in a whirl. "It wasn't Ara! It was me. I made her do it."

"Stop it." Eve immediately started to unwind her hand from mine. "Don't you dare take the blame for that."

Avery sneered, then his expression became malicious. "Their faces are all over the media."

Miles met my eyes with his. To my surprise, he didn't

appear betrayed. "What does it matter?" he asked. "They're good people; you've seen that."

"Good people don't kill security agents," Avery said, looking from my face to the uniform. "Tell them who you are!" he snapped.

"Avery, stop it!" Cal demanded. "They wouldn't kill someone." But when he said it, he didn't sound certain.

I looked over at Emi. Her eyes were filling with tears. "Hanson?" Her voice trembled as she spoke.

"Don't call him that!" Avery yelled. "His real name is Adam. They've been using us since the beginning."

Miles shook his head unbelievingly. "Criminals don't go into a Red Zone risking their lives to help a scientist."

"Explain the uniform then!"

I put my hands up as a gesture of innocence. "He tried to kill us," I said slowly.

"I don't believe—"

"Shut up!" Emi screamed. "I want to hear what he says!"

Tears formed in my eyes. I had broken my promise to her. I had let her down.

"He killed my, my boss, Linda, at the Border Station earlier that day," I explained, trying desperately to sound calm. "If you could, I'd let you search my memories. You would see."

"He didn't cause the breach," Eve said, slipping the agent's small black weapon with the button from her jacket pocket. Everyone drew back instinctively, but Emi didn't move a muscle.

"He was going to kill Adam," Eve went on, holding the weapon up for everyone to see. "But I didn't let him." She was crying. "I didn't know what else to do."

Aimee stood up and was by Eve's side in a flash, pulling her into a hug. "Fuck you!" she yelled at Avery. "You have no idea what she's been through!"

Emi jumped across the fire and grabbed the security agent's weapon from Eve's hand before anyone could stop her.

"Emi, stop!" Cal screamed. "You could kill them!"

Emi whipped around to face Miles, Avery, and Cal, holding the weapon in front of herself, outstretched toward them. "No," she said. Her voice no longer shook, and there weren't tears in her eyes. She sounded strong. "No, it wouldn't kill them. They're like me."

The three agents exchanged glances, and Miles merely nodded his head, finally understanding.

"It won't kill them," Emi repeated. "But it could kill *you*." She shook the weapon at them threateningly. "Do you want to die?" she screamed. "Would you turn in my friend? Would you turn me in? Would you kill us?" I'd never seen her look so angry. The happy little girl who sat across the fire with her stick was threatening to kill these men. "I'll do it! If you make a move, I'll kill you!" Her voice faltered on the last words. She didn't want to kill anyone.

"Emi." Eve tried to sound as calm as she could. "Emi, please give me the weapon." But Emi didn't let go.

I understood what she was trying to do. It was a way for us to escape. Aimee clutched her device protectively in her hands, and we didn't need anything else. We could do it, but would the agents follow us? They had the autonome. They could easily track us using drones, though they'd never be able to access the signals from our Monitors because they didn't exist.

"Hanson," Miles began, then corrected himself, "I mean, Adam. I believe what you said, and I don't believe you would harm us. Though I wouldn't blame you if you did." He glared at Avery.

Avery scowled but didn't say a word. For a moment, he appeared worried. I imagined him thinking of his husband and what he'd do to get back to him. Probably the same thing Emi was doing to save Eve, Aimee, and me.

"You're going to let us go," Emi continued, the strength coming back to her voice. "You're going to let us go, and you're not going to follow us."

I glanced at Eve. Her fists were clenched nervously. I

reached out to touch Emi's arm, and she flinched when my hand met her shoulder, but she didn't trigger the weapon. "Emi," I said softly. "Let's go."

She nodded her head, and I looked at Eve again as she took back the weapon. This time, she met my gaze, and she understood. We were going to leave. We were going to run, and Aimee was going to come with us.

Emi took the first step backward, her eyes still on the men, then she turned around and shot past us, running as fast as she could.

"Wait!" Cal called.

"We're not going to hurt you or turn you in!" Miles added, yelling as loud as he could. "We want to help you! Adam, remember?"

I stopped in my tracks. If Miles wasn't lying, he knew people that had the ability to help us, to change our identity chips. Eve and I could be free of our lives in Vegas and help Emi find her sister, if she was still alive. I had to believe she was.

Emi stopped when she noticed I wasn't following her anymore, and the others soon followed. We were standing on the suburb street at dusk, the men near the front of the house.

"If you go out there," Cal said, "someone will notice you. They will turn you in without a second thought. They will kill you! They will kill all of you . . ."

"Please, let me help you!" Miles was looking directly at me. "I want to help you."

"*Non, c'est pas vrai. Je ne le crois pas,*" Emi said quickly in French. I didn't understand, but I guessed she didn't trust them. She'd told me men who were mistrusting and made rash decisions were the real reason her brother was dead. She couldn't stand to lose him again. She couldn't stand to lose me, and I'd do whatever it took to make sure she was okay. I didn't fully trust Miles, but deep down, I wanted to believe the man who stood in front of us, offering to sacrifice his life to save ours. Even if I had my helmet and we all changed clothes, we wouldn't be able to hide our faces. Eve and I would be recognized; Cal was right. We'd be turned in, and I'd be put on death row for impersonating a security agent. For killing a man. I wouldn't let Eve take the blame for it, but that was only if the State didn't access our memories, which wasn't a given. They could; they had the power to. It was against the law, but that wasn't to say they wouldn't do it. Eve and I were part of a murder investigation. Anything could happen to us. Anything at all.

Still, it was a risk. I wasn't able to tell what Avery's intentions were; maybe he just meant to threaten us. If only he'd listen to what I said and trust that we never meant to hurt anyone, but that was a big "if." He had the ability to send signals through his Monitor; Eve hadn't disabled that. He could notify Defense and Security that he found the two people wanted for the murder of the man who'd tried to kill me. He could sentence me to death in a matter of seconds. Then again, Eve could end his life in less.

I turned toward her. Her eyes were fixed rigidly on Avery. "Don't do it," she told him, her voice stern.

"Is your name even Ara?" he dared to ask.

Her eyes narrowed into slits, and Aimee lunged forward at the man in anger, but Eve grabbed her arm to stop her before she did anything she regretted.

Avery took a step away from the other men in our direction. "I could do it," he said. "I could notify the agency you're here. They'd find you. You wouldn't be able to hide."

Please be empty threats, I thought. *I don't want to see you die.* Out of everyone in the group, he seemed to be the one with the most hope and the most compassion. Maybe I was too quick to judge who he was.

Cal glared at his friend. "You wouldn't dare. We volunteered to be a part of this rescue mission to save lives, not end them."

"Like they did," Avery said accusingly of Eve and me, his muscles tense.

Miles stepped briskly in front of him, shoving him backward with one swift movement. "What if it was you, huh?

What if it was your life on the line? What if it was Scott's?"

Scott was his husband. Would Avery do anything to save him? Was he acting this way to make sure he saw him again?

Miles took another step closer to his friend until he was face to face with him, his expression hardened in anger. His nostrils flared, veins popped on his neck, and his jaw clenched tightly. Usually, he looked to be around my age, 23, but he seemed to age twenty years in that moment.

"Anything can happen!" he shouted. "Anything! What about all the death we've witnessed? Would you willingly cause more suffering? And what about me, huh, Avery? Do you think I expected to lose the love of my life to this fucking nightmare we're living in? Adam and Ara are trying to save that girl's life! Someone tried to kill them! In this world, anything can happen. You of all people should know that."

"Don't you dare bring that up." Avery looked like he was ready to attack.

Miles backed away and started laughing uncontrollably. "'Cause it's all about you, right?" He doubled over, then suddenly stood up, full of furious intensity. "Do you think this man was always a respectable medical agent?" he scoffed, regarding everyone but Avery. "Do you know what he did?"

"*Don't.*" Avery's tone was severe.

Miles ignored him completely. "He used to perform *the surgery*." He didn't need to say anything else. We all knew what he meant; it was considered one of the biggest crimes in our society: the surgery to remove a Monitor.

Suddenly, the medical agent's fist slammed into the side of Miles's head, hitting him with such force that his body went limp and smashed into the ground with a loud thud. Cal was immediately on Avery, shoving him to the ground to stop him, but he was the strongest of the three men. Cal didn't stand a chance. All at once, he was on his back, Avery with his knee to Cal's chest and his fists around the redhead's throat. Miles lay unconscious in the grass next to them.

Emi screamed and ran toward Miles. "What have you done?"

"Emi, stop!" Eve tried to grab Emi to keep her away from the fight, but Emi ducked past and fell to her knees next to Miles, pulling his head into her lap. "He's bleeding." Her face was red, like she was trying to stop herself from crying. "Why is he bleeding so much?"

"Look at what you did!" Cal choked, pulling furiously at Avery's hands as he tried to suck air into his lungs. "Look! T-that's . . . Your—friend! H-how could—" He couldn't finish his sentence. Avery was suffocating him.

Eve held the security agent's weapon in her hand. "Try to stop him, Adam. Please. I don't want to—"

Before she said another word, I was racing toward Cal and Avery. Cal's nails dug so hard into Avery's forearms, they were bleeding, but he still didn't let go of Cal, not until my boot connected with his ribcage. Immediately, his grip loosened on Cal's throat, giving him time to suck in enough oxygen to keep himself from blacking out on the lawn. He lay there for a minute heaving while I shoved Avery to the ground to distract him.

"You going to kill me like you killed that agent?" Avery's muscles flexed under his shirt. "They showed images of his body and that huge bloody hole in the back of his head where his Monitor used to be!"

"I didn't kill him!" I screamed. "He was going to murder me! He killed my friend!" Tears fell from my eyes as my fist connected with his nose and a loud snap told me I broke it on impact.

Cal pushed himself up off the ground and moved quickly next to Miles's body. His hands shot to the man's throat, checking for a pulse.

"Why is he bleeding so much?" Emi said in between sobs.

"His nose," Cal explained as he tore a section of gauze from a roll inside his belt pouch to press against the safety agent's nose to stop the bleeding. "It's broken, Emi." His head shot back at Avery as the man stood up across from me, still ready to fight despite his broken nose and bruised ribs. "You could have killed him!"

"Fuck you! I can't die here! I have to make it back to my husband . . . I have to." Just when Avery lunged forward to attack me again, Aimee raced up behind him, and her tablet connected so hard with his skull, it shattered the screen. Avery stumbled toward me, but I caught his body before he fell face-first onto the pavement of the deserted suburb street.

Aimee yelped and let the device fall to the pavement, her hands shaking violently. "Please tell me I didn't kill him!"

I laid his body on the ground as gently as I could—he was a lot heavier than I expected—and hurriedly felt for his pulse. To my relief, his heart was still beating, and hot air emanated from his mouth. He was still alive. I wanted to hate him when I looked over to see Miles still unconscious in the grass, but I couldn't. The man didn't want to kill us. He could easily have done it if he tried. He merely wanted to make it back to Vegas alive and go home to his husband.

"Are you okay?" Eve asked as she crouched next to me, shoving the weapon deep into her pocket. She seemed conflicted. "I wanted to use it, Adam. I wanted so badly to use it. It took everything I had not to."

"It's okay," I muttered. "We're okay."

She hugged me in response, and I wanted nothing more than to keep holding onto her. After a moment, I stood up and pulled Avery's body back over to the lawn to lay him down.

"We need to leave him behind," Cal said. "Wherever we go, we can't take him with us. It's a risk."

"*Soit bien,* Miles, *s'il te plait,*" Emi murmured, begging Miles to be okay. She held his hand while Cal pulled a device from his belt and held it over his friend's face. A blue light shown from the bottom when he pressed a button, repairing the damage Avery had inflicted.

Aimee sat down on the curb and buried her face in her hands. "It's done. We're done."

Eve peered worriedly at me. Aimee's device was destroyed, used as a weapon to save my life. She'd no longer be able to watch over the seismic activity in the area. Her colleagues could from a distance, but the readings wouldn't be as accurate as hers because they weren't as close to the epicenter of the activity below the Earth's surface.

The only thing we had was the autonome. "Is there any way you can tap into the autonome's system to read the activity?" I asked Eve.

"I'm not sure," she said truthfully. "If it has a strong enough signal, possibly." She sat next to Aimee to try and comfort her. "Where is the nearest geological research facility? One with the equipment you need?"

I walked away to check on Miles.

"He's stable," Cal said, looking up at me. "He'll be okay." Miles's face no longer looked disfigured. It looked like nothing had happened to him at all, but the blood smeared down Cal's hands, arms, and shirt told me otherwise.

Emi moved to sit next to me, then buried her face in my chest. "*J'ai peur*, Adam. *C'était effrayant. J'ai pensé que . . . qu'Avery va te tuerait.*"

I understood enough to know what she meant. "You thought I was going to die?"

"*Oui*," she whispered. Her voice was muddled by the fabric of my uniform.

"Impossible." I wiped a tear from her face. "You'll never get rid of me."

Emi tilted her head up to look at me and grinned for a moment, then it faded. "Don't make promises you can't keep."

"Emi . . ." My shoulders fell, and Cal frowned.

I repeated her name and held her freckled face in mine. "I promise you I'll stay with you until I die."

"So did Peter. Then they killed him."

CHAPTER 14

"Dammit!" Eve punched the dash of the autonome.

"How can I help?" Aimee asked as Eve rolled the window down and started yelling about useless satellites and network connections.

Miles laughed next to me while we sat in the grass. "It looks good on the outside"—he motioned to his nose—"but the headache is killer." "You know," he continued, "if we weren't stuck here with a useless machine that won't turn on, if we had a way to oversee the quakes, and if Avery wasn't tied up in the living room, this whole situation wouldn't be too bad."

I chuckled. I understood what he was trying to say. We'd finally met people who had similar goals, weren't consumed with their images and reputations, and were willing to help people even if it put them at risk, or so it seemed, yet we were in the worst situation most of us had ever been in. Emi having to flee her home and lose her sister because radicals wanted them dead, and not to mention Eve losing her former life, surpassed our problems, but I was tired of being worried and scared.

"Don't forget to add to our situation that Ara and I are wanted for murder, and Emi is considered a disgrace to society because she's an Untouchable. Am I missing anything?"

"A lot." Miles's expression turned dark, and he went quiet for a moment, then said, "But let's not talk about that."

"There's no way for me to overwrite the signals if the fucking thing is offline!" Eve swung herself out of the autonome and slammed the door violently, kicking it as she did.

Right as Eve banged the door shut, Cal stepped out of the house onto the porch. "It's been reported as stolen." He motioned to the machine. "I saw it. That's why it's been turned off. The media has photos of me, Avery, Miles, and Aimee being sent out through the Monitors, along with information about where the autonome was last seen. They're listing us as missing persons. We're presumed dead."

When Eve had disabled the Monitors' and autonome's ability to receive incoming signals, she'd also disabled their ability to be tracked.

The sick, twisting sensation in the pit of my stomach returned, and I had to shut my eyes for a moment. Eve and I had not only sealed our fates but the fates of the men that were helping us. What would their families think?

Aimee's eyebrows knit together. "That doesn't make any sense. I sent them the signal about the quake. I can't send a signal if I'm dead."

"That was three days ago," Cal said, frowning. "Of course they'd presume us dead. It's against the law to mess with the Monitors' signals. It incites the death penalty. People rarely get charged with it, if ever. When the signals stop and a person can no longer be located, it usually means the Monitor was compromised, and the person was killed."

These were things we knew but didn't think about because we typically didn't need to.

"What do we do?" Aimee asked, stepping out of the machine. "We're sitting ducks. Unless one of us sends out a signal, we're stuck here. Public transport is only running for evacuation purposes. Dead people and murderers don't fit that bill. If we try and get into the city on our own that way or on foot, Officers will immediately stop us. There's no way we won't be detected."

"Unless we're smart about our movements," Eve offered.

That wasn't going to cut it. It was too much of a risk. "Miles?" I looked at the man. There was still blood smeared on his shirt collar and the ends of his hair. He was a wreck, and I was about to ask him to risk his career and life as he knew it. "You told me about someone you know that could help us. Do you know if you can truly trust this person?"

"Absolutely. She's my stepsister, but she doesn't exist as far as the government is concerned. She was presumed dead at eighteen and has been operating under the radar for about four years now with a different name. But I don't see how she could help at this point. You're wanted for murder, Adam."

My face fell, but then I had an idea. "Can you get access to an autonome? We need a way out of here."

While I waited for a response, Cal, Aimee, and Eve stood near the front of the house, speaking quickly amongst themselves.

"Is he really your friend, Cal? Friends don't try to murder other friends. The way he looked at you when he had you on the ground—" Eve shuddered.

"He is. He told me he didn't alert the authorities. He didn't send out a signal. He's just worried about his husband, about Scott. He probably thinks Avery's dead."

Miles coughed and rubbed his throat, which still looked sore, drawing my attention back to him. "I think she'd be able to help us, but where would we go? The minute any one of us goes outside the autonome, we run the risk of being recognized."

"Only by those with Monitors," I clarified. "Or those who have immediate access to Screens. But what about the people who don't have either of those things? They're the ones the Regime doesn't care about. Do you think any Untouchables are being rescued and sent to New Anchorage or evacuated to the northern cities?"

He nodded. "You're right. Anyone with a Monitor would most likely recognize us, and my guess is they wouldn't waste any time reporting us. But the Untouchables wouldn't care who we are. I think they'd want our help, especially with how bad it's gotten. We were told by our agency that the groups of them in Vegas that were contacted refused our aide, but I didn't believe that for one minute. I don't think anyone tried to contact them at all in any of the Red Zones. How could they lower themselves to that level?"

"Exactly. The Untouchables are the ones that need the most help. So many of them don't have the means to try and escape. They wouldn't have enough food to last evacuating, and they'd have to do so on foot." They weren't allowed to use public or private transportation.

"But it's still risky. If we continue with the plan to go to Cincinnati, we'll be going headfirst into an area surrounded by Defense and Security. They'll most likely be concentrated around the major stations and highways leading in and out of the city to try and regulate evacuation . . ." He stood up and started pacing back and forth, his brows furrowed in concentration. "We could find ways around that. The autonomes are capable of going off road, and we could go as far as we could with them and continue on foot, if needed, and leave them somewhere we could bring groups of people back to for evacuation. There are also a lot of abandoned roads and outlets that are rarely used anymore, with autonomes being restricted to highways; we could take advantage of those. I've had to use them in other cities for search and rescue."

"As long as we're careful, I think we can make this work."

He looked at me, hope lighting up his eyes. "I think we can too."

Along the skyline behind the continuous row of houses in the quiet suburb, the faint orange and pink glow from the earlier sunset mixed with the blue-black shadows of the approaching night. Another unexpected day was nearing its end, but we were just beginning to plan our next step. The others had agreed to what Miles and I had come up with, but before we attempted to get anywhere near Cincinnati and try to help as many Untouchables as we could, we needed to be aware of what was happening with the natural disasters. Eve said she believed she could tap into the seismic recording system if she had access to a signal system with a high enough bandwidth. We'd looked for abandoned devices or anything that might work in some of the homes, but nothing was powerful enough, and the connection to the Internet was down, of course. Eve needed that to get into the seismic recording network for Aimee.

Wireless was down because power outside major cities had been shut off to conserve energy for core functions and the repair of damaged sections of the Dome. The core functions of the country included the Monitors. Every device needed connection to satellite networks through electromagnetic radio waves, and the satellites were maintained by facilities in St. Louis, New Anchorage, and Vegas. The system was strong, but it could fail. It could always fail. And if it did, the Monitors would be useless. They'd be nothing but a bunch of wires in the back of the head without the signals powering them.

I thought about what Aimee had said at the outpost when Eve had told her she wished she could turn them off and let people see what life was like without them. Aimee said people would lose their minds, and I believed that was true. Most didn't know anything but the Monitors. As much as I hated them, if they lost function all at once, it would be catastrophic.

But that wasn't our problem. Yet.

Our solution to the power outage was to get as close as we could to Cincinnati without endangering ourselves so that Eve could hack into the monitoring system Aimee needed. Miles's stepsister was going to send an autonome: a black market steal from a high-profile socialite who kept their fortune by providing high-class services like autonomes and medicine to people who were desperate, just like we were.

The autonome would not only serve the purpose of getting us close to Cincinnati and helping people once we knew what we were up against, but it also had a strong enough signal system for Eve to use it to gain access to the seismic monitoring system once we had Internet again.

We felt good about the plan. Our only skepticism lay in our

newfound distrust of Avery. We couldn't be certain he hadn't sent a signal to the Security Agency. Eve had disabled his ability to send out radio waves through his Monitor, like the rest of us, but the damage could've already been done.

While we waited for the autonome, we moved our base several miles away from our previous location to an almost identical suburb, just in case anyone came looking for us. Emi stood next to me in the spacious living room, much larger than the last, frequently peering out the curtains of the bay window at the street lit up by the unending row of solar lamps.

"Miles said it should be here soon," I told her, and she stepped back from the window, letting the curtain fall in its place and making the room dark once more.

We took precautions to make sure our presence wasn't known in the home to anyone from the outside. Curtains and blinds were shut, all doors and windows were locked, and everyone besides whoever's turn it was to watch for the autonome was to stay away from the windows. The lights wouldn't turn on even if we wanted them to because of the power outage, and the owners didn't use solar or wind energy for backup. Most citizens couldn't afford to or chose to spend their money on other things.

"I'm sorry for what I said earlier," Emi said suddenly, her voice low enough for only me to hear. "I didn't mean to compare you to my brother, Peter, I just . . ." Her voice shook. "I don't want you to die."

I didn't want to compare her to the little girl I saw on the Screen at the outpost, but I was terrified of losing Emi. Because of that, I understood why she was afraid to lose me.

"Bastard!" Miles's voice pierced the air like a shotgun. I spun around in an instant to see his shadowy figure standing above Avery, who sat at a table in the kitchen, his arms and legs tightly bound.

"I didn't do—" Miles slapped Avery across the face, cutting him off. The sound was so loud, I could almost feel the sting on my own skin.

"Damn you!"

"Miles, calm down," Cal warned.

"What happened?" Emi asked Eve, standing in the living room away from the men. Eve pointed at the kitchen window, and Emi walked over. I followed, lifting a blind carefully once I reached the window.

One street over, in the shadows cast by the solar lamps, an autonome was parked outside a brick house. I let the blinds fall and looked over at Miles. "What are you doing?" I demanded. "Why are we wasting our time? The autonome is here."

Miles pursed his lips and shook his head. "Look again," he said in a low voice, glaring at Avery.

Emi had already lifted another blind. She gasped, terrified, and looked at me. "What do we do?"

Standing at a front window of the brick house, peering in with a flashlight, were two figures. One was dressed in an all-black uniform, including leather boots and gloves, and wore a sleek, rounded helmet that made them look more like a machine than a human being. It was a security agent. The other figure was a woman, who appeared to be in her thirties, and had short, buzzed blonde hair. Were they looking for us? Everyone else was gone.

I panicked and drew back from the window instantly. *The fire.* The thought hit me like a train. If no one put out the fire we had burning in the back yard, the agent and the woman would come across it.

"Don't worry," Aimee said, seeming to read my mind. "They won't find a trace of us." She sat at the table on the other side of Avery, studying him while she spoke. "We poured water over the fire. They won't catch it. You can thank Ara for that."

Eve shrugged. "You can never be too safe."

Miles didn't seem to hear anything anyone said. He was fuming. "I should've listened to my gut. I knew you sent the signal, you prick."

"I know I said I would," Avery said quickly. The anger that consumed him earlier was gone from his voice. The only thing that remained was fear. "But I didn't, I swear. Miles, you and Cal are my friends. You know I wouldn't—"

"Then explain that!" Miles motioned out the window sharply. As soon as the two individuals finished checking the street they were on, they'd be on us, and we were in one of the first houses in that row.

"Miles, the autonome!"

"I already told you, it's theirs, Ad—"

"I know! Did you tell your sister to stall the one she sent us?" If an autonome showed up outside this house, they'd want to know why.

Miles glared again at Avery, then stepped away from him over to me. "Yes. It's a couple miles away from here. She's waiting for my go-ahead to send it."

I breathed a sigh of relief.

"I'm sorry. We were so close to getting out of here."

"Listen to me!" Avery yelled, interrupting us. "I don't know who they are, I swear! Listen to me, please!"

"Shut up," Cal insisted, keeping his voice low. "We need to stop making noise."

I looked at Miles. Emi had her arms around my waist in a tight hug, breathing quickly. "What do we do?" I asked.

"Now we wait."

Three more houses and the woman and security agent would be on us. It was only a matter of time before they were shining their flashlights through the windows and knocking on the door.

We moved quickly. Miles, Cal, and Aimee drug Avery up the stairs into one of the second-floor bedrooms. Eve, Emi, and I went into another.

"Just in case anything happens," Aimee had told us. "We will distract them while you escape. Don't look back, don't think about us, just go." She took Emi's hand in hers. "You *will* escape, for all of us."

From what I could tell, we were in a child's room, but I had little to go on. Besides a small bed, there was a less complex and immersive version of the Screens that made up the invisible outpost in the Vegas desert, though this one still took up the entire length of the wall opposite us. I thought about how impersonal the room was, but that wasn't strange for our society. All of your memories, who your friends were, the music you listened to, the things that made you laugh—all of that came from the Monitors. Why would you need anything physical? Anything real.

We sat across from the Screen on the bed. The only thing that gave away that the room might've belonged to a child was the stuffed animal tucked under the soft linen sheets.

I had the sudden urge to crawl underneath them and lay down. If I wasn't absolutely terrified, I might. It felt like it had been days since I'd slept, though I hadn't done much of that even when I was alone.

Emi looked exhausted as well. She pulled a pillow close to her and let her head fall onto it, then drew her knees up to her chest and closed her eyes. I thought for a moment that she was going to cry, but she was much stronger than I was when I was her age. Instead, she asked me to tell her a story. But what could I say to her? We were right back where we were the night Aimee detected the strong energy readings from the New Madrid fault zone.

"We'll be okay," Eve had told us as we'd walked up the stairs to the room to hide. "As long as we don't make any loud noises, we'll be okay." I watched her now; she was sitting at the desk in the room, fumbling with a stress ball, intently watching the street below through a slit in the window blinds.

"What kind of story?" I finally asked Emi, my stomach twisting at the thought of how close the two figures were getting to us.

My eyes had adjusted to the minimal light, but Emi still looked like a dark shadow on the bed, the shape of her curly hair her only recognizable feature. "T—tell me about your life," she said, breathing in and out deeply to try and calm herself.

I wanted to tell her something happy to distract her from

the security agent and woman making their way toward the house, but could I even think of something happy to share? I'd have to go way back to my childhood. The last time I remembered feeling happy—really, truly happy—and excited about the future was when I was with Aaron, the boy I met in middle school who taught me about language, about literature and writing, and about what it meant to be alive. He reminded me of her.

"I was walking from the school building several blocks away from the orphanage I grew up in," I started. "No one bothered me then. They were too busy listening to broadcasts through their Monitors or talking to people who were thousands of miles away from them that they'd never meet."

They were all generally alone, but to them, they felt they were always surrounded. It wasn't until I met Aaron that I knew why my mother did everything she could to make sure I wasn't forced into the same life as everyone else. Because of her, I grew up wondering why I was different, but it was that difference that made me see clearer in the end and made me realize just how wrong the social structure we were living in was. There were good people, and the world could be beautiful, but our priorities were misguided, and most of us didn't genuinely care about much of anything besides what other people thought of us.

"As I walked back to the orphanage, I kept my head down and went unnoticed by everyone, except one kid who looked to be around my age. He was coming out of an abandoned building in the run-down part of the city where I grew up. The officials at the orphanage always told us not to go near the abandoned factories, that people who were dangerous could be hiding there. One lady told me a group of Untouchables lived in a particular building, and she made up stories, telling me they were like savages, living in their own filth and teaching their children how to become criminals and ultimately work to destroy the system that was the Regime. I pictured people in tattered clothes with matted hair and wild eyes who spoke languages no one else could understand and who would kill me if I ever saw them.

"But the boy I saw climbing out of a window on the ground floor of the abandoned factory didn't look like that at all. He was tall for his age and muscular, with dirty blonde hair that came down to his shoulders, much like Miles's, and he had dark brown eyes and a smile that could warm an entire room. He was inviting, and nothing about him looked dangerous. He caught me staring at him as I tried to figure out if it was possible that he could be a part of the group Ms. Langley had described."

"He sounds wonderful," Emi interrupted. "*Aaron,*" she said his name aloud. "I don't know anyone with that name, but I already like him."

Talking about him helped calm my nerves, and I even managed to smile. "He was funny, and reminded me a lot of you. He saw things differently." I'd always wondered how my life would've turned out if he hadn't shown me what it really meant to be an Untouchable.

"After he caught me staring at him, he waved me over. I ran away without saying a word but took the same path home after school the next day. He was waiting there for me again, but I didn't stop. The next day, I did the same thing. I was afraid of what he represented, but my curiosity was trying to overpower that. He was one of the first people that had taken notice of me. I was so used to being ignored, it was a shock, to be honest . . . I didn't see him the day I finally worked up the courage to say something, but he saw me. He was hiding in an alley across the street and jumped out as I passed. I nearly pissed my pants, but when he started to laugh, I couldn't help but join in. I don't know how to describe it, but Aaron had a way of making me feel safe—like I actually belonged somewhere.

"We started meeting at the same spot after school every day. The workers at the orphanage didn't mind if I didn't show up. As long as I was there by curfew, they couldn't have cared less where I was at. So I got to know an Untouchable. I was fascinated by him. He could speak four different languages other than English: French, Russian, Norwegian, and Italian. He spent hours every day writing about people he met and the things he saw in and outside the city. It was with Aaron that I first left Vegas. We took a Tram to Sedona and spent the day exploring the red canyons in the city. We even swam in a stream that ran the length of one of the cliffs. It was the first time I experienced an area that was natural. There weren't many people, just a few exercising through the canyon here and there, but we were pretty much alone, surrounded by red rock and the desert. I never wanted to leave. I felt like I could breathe out there. I didn't see a Screen, I couldn't hear the buzz of the Monitors, and people didn't move in masses toward their offices. It was peaceful."

"I always loved being outside," Emi said. "I think I'd die if I couldn't feel grass beneath my feet."

"Aaron was the same way."

"What happened to him?" Eve asked. She'd stopped fumbling with the stress ball and was listening to the story.

"He disappeared," I said, the happiness I'd felt talking about him quickly fading. "I waited for him one day, and he never came. I stayed there all night, but I never dared to go into the abandoned building. Aaron said there were certain people that wouldn't accept someone from the outside, someone who was still as connected to the Regime as I was, despite my lack of a Monitor. He told me the Untouchables would resent me for trying to live in normal society." But he never did. He understood I was lost in the world and just trying to find a way to survive.

"I waited for him for weeks, but I never saw him again. Eventually, I gave up. I should've gone into the building, but I was so young. I was scared. More than anything, I didn't want to face the probability that my best friend had been killed by people who despised the Untouchables and sought to remove their presence from society altogether . . ." I trailed off as Eve stood up from the chair and risked a glance out the window.

"They're two houses away from us," she said, sitting back

down quickly. "We have to be quiet now, okay?"

We nodded. "We're going to make it through this," I told Emi, but she didn't say anything. She grabbed my hand, and I could feel just how badly she was shaking.

Eve's brows were furrowed in concentration. She was listening intently to the Monitor, the earpiece pushed firmly into her left ear. After a moment, her face lit up, and she sucked in a sharp breath of air. "Adam," she whispered so low, I could barely hear her. She was trying to be quiet for Emi, who'd fallen asleep. Her body had finally shut down out of sheer exhaustion and the built-up anxiety and stress.

"Adam," Eve murmured once more. "You have to listen to this. I didn't realize what it was at first, but I found it. Adam, I found *them.*"

The Untouchables. That had to be what she meant! I'd searched for hours and hours, hoping I'd come across the station Emi had told us about, hoping I'd hear something that would make sense of the beliefs Emi had described. Something about the omnipotent being.

Eve pulled the earpiece from her head, making sure not to make any noise, then quickly handed it to me. I shoved it in, and the first thing I heard was the name Bridget Klein.

"We're interrupting our broadcast of the debate here just outside Cincinnati to talk to you about a group of Untouchables from the Dayton area. As you already know, the media has nothing to do with the coverage of our people. Because of this, there was no alert about a mass killing in the area this past week. Late Wednesday night, two radicals by the names of Nadim Aras and Rei Hanley decided to take the central debate around the cause of these natural disasters to a drastic height, one that cost the lives of their group."

"It's terrible," the woman lamented. "They killed the majority of their group, and those that did it actually thought they were doing the right thing."

"Sometimes people do bad things because they believe they are doing them for all the right reasons, but I can't forgive this, Kena. I don't know what else to say," said another voice.

"I know," Kena said, her voice coming in and out with the varying strength of the signal. "If you are a surviving member of this group from the Dayton area, please listen very closely to what we are about to tell you. Spencer, please."

"We have an urgent notice to send out on behalf of a good friend, Bridget Klein. We mentioned her name earlier," Spencer pressed on. "She arrived at our base only hours ago, coming straight from Dayton. If you have been in touch with a girl by the name of Emi Klein, please send us a message as soon as you are able. Emi went missing after the internal raid by the radicals last Wednesday night and has been gone since. Bridget is here with us. Emi, if you are listening, be careful. It's dangerous here. We can't give you our location. People are listening. People that could destroy us. But please, Emi, Bridget is here. If you can find us, if you can send us a message somehow, please do. I repeat, Emi, Bridget is here. God speed."

I looked at the shadowy form curled up in the bed, her hair sticking up like a mane framing her face. Her eyes were closed, and she looked so peaceful. I wanted to wake her immediately and tell her that her sister was alive, but I also didn't want to get her hopes up. All we knew was that they were outside Cincinnati. They could be anywhere, and if the authorities were tracking them, they had to be well hidden.

"Eve," I said so low I could barely hear myself over my heart beating out of my chest.

"What is it?" she asked worriedly.

"Emi's sister is alive," I whispered. "She's outside the city with the group on the radio."

Eve dropped the stress ball on the ground as her mouth fell open, but it didn't make any sound to wake Emi as it hit the soft carpet. "She's alive?"

"Yes. What did they say when you were listening?"

"They were going on about religion. They mentioned Judgement Day. I thought they might say something about— I don't know. It was a stupid thought, but I think my dream had something to do with all of this."

I shook my head. "That's impossible."

She didn't respond, just looked out the window again.

I put the earpiece back in. I told Eve it was impossible, and that made sense. But the natural disasters didn't, did they? I wanted to listen to the broadcast all night long, hoping they'd reveal something.

"We are working on getting Bridget into the studio, but she's having difficulty. She's eight months pregnant. Can you believe it, Kena? Emi was going to be an aunt."

"Is, Spencer. She *is* going to be an aunt," Kena corrected her co-host, then added, "Emi Klein, that's her name. If you're just tuning into this broadcast signal, be advised that we are looking for a young girl by the name of Emi Klein. I will not describe her here, in case anyone is listening who'd use the information to find her and detain her, or worse. Emi, if you are listening, your sister is nearby."

A muffled sound came through the broadcast: a voice speaking with the hosts. I couldn't hear everything they said, only snippets. "Please . . . if she's listening . . . hear my voice." I couldn't make out who it was, but it was a male's voice. He sounded anxious.

Kena's voice came back through the earpiece. "We're going to bring on Bridget's boyfriend, who'd like to say a few words to Emi, if you are out there listening."

A crackling noise followed as the microphone was transferred from Kena to Bridget's boyfriend. "Emi, everything is going to be okay. Your sister is safe. She's strong, just like you. We *will* find you, Emi. I swear my life on it."

I strained my ears listening to his voice. He sounded familiar, like an echo of someone I heard long ago. Then it hit me.

"You worry too much, Adam. Everything is going to be okay, I promise. You just have to get through this, and then you'll never have to see them again. You can be whoever you want, do whatever you want. You could be a writer, you know? You love it; you haven't stopped with the pen and paper since we've been practicing. You're going to make a change. I

believe in you."

It was Aaron. His voice was distorted, deeper and not as innocent, but it was him. He still had the same uplifting tone he had when I knew him. I couldn't believe it. I thought he'd probably been picked up by the authorities and charged with some crime he didn't commit, then thrown in jail. That, or something terrible had happened. I always chose the first scenario because it was less painful than coming to terms with the fact that I'd lost another person in my life that I cared for.

"Adam, what's going on? What are they saying?" Eve asked when she saw the surprised look that came and was swiftly replaced by a saddened expression on my face. It was like I was standing outside the abandoned building all over again, waiting for a friend that would never come. A chill ran down my spine, and I had to shake my head to draw myself away from my thoughts. It didn't matter who he was or who he'd become. All that mattered was getting Emi back to her sister, safe and alive.

Eve touched my hand. "Did something happen? Talk to me, please."

I blinked a few times, just to make sure I wasn't dreaming. But I wasn't. It was real. A ghost from my past had reappeared. I was confused at first, but the more I thought about it, the more it made sense. Aaron had always spoken about getting away from the West Coast and seeing more of the Regime. He wanted to learn about the various groups of Untouchables, what they believed, and what they taught their children. He wanted a change, but he wanted it for all the right reasons. He wanted to experience as much as life could offer. I, on the other hand, wanted to forget about my past and had spent the better part of my youth trying to erase it.

I took a deep breath, trying to calm myself. I wanted to scream. I had so many questions for Aaron, for Bridget, Emi, Kena, and Spencer. I wanted to understand, more than I ever had, everything about our past that the Regime had buried.

"I know him, Bridget's boyfriend," I said to Eve finally.

"Who's Bridget?"

But I never got the chance to respond.

Bang! Bang! Bang!

There were three knocks on the door, so loud it sounded as though the person could punch straight through the wood. My heart stopped, my breathing hitched, and I suddenly became aware of just how loud my breathing was, and that of Emi and Eve as well.

Please leave, please just leave. I'd just found out that Emi's sister was alive. We could find her, and Emi could continue living the life she loved and never wanted to give up. *Please let me save her.*

There was another knock at the door, and the woman with the buzzed blonde hair spoke in a clear, firm voice, with no emotion in her tone. She called repeatedly, asking if someone was here. Was she waiting for one of us to break out of fear?

"There's no way they know we're here," Eve whispered, but she was frozen still in the chair. She thought that if she moved, they'd see her, even though we were shrouded in darkness on the second floor of the house. "They won't know unless Avery decides to make our presence known. If it means he'll get back to his husband, he might try and turn us in. They'd let him go if he did."

"Miles would stop him before he could."

"He tried to stop Avery last time, and it almost cost him his life."

Miles wouldn't let that happen again. I was certain of that. "He was just taken off guard. He thought Avery was his friend." That friendship was destroyed in a matter of seconds.

I shifted my gaze to Emi. I couldn't see her face well enough in the low light to see if she was awake, but her body was still. I was surprised she hadn't woken up when the woman banged on the front door, seemingly with all the force she had, and when she called out asking if anyone was still here. Her voice was like a shotgun in the ringing silence. Then, I realized I was wrong.

Emi's breathing was no longer steady but came out short and ragged, and her body quivered slightly. She was crying, which meant she was awake, and she knew our group was no longer alone.

I moved closer to her, reaching out my hand to touch her shoulder. "It's okay. We're going to be okay." She didn't respond, and I knew that I had to give her something to focus on that would make her forget that we were in danger, if only for a moment. I had to give her hope.

"Listen to me," I said hastily, not knowing how much time I had before something bad happened again. "Your sister is alive."

Her blue-grey eyes widened while I spoke, and her mouth fell open in disbelief. "H—how?"

I held the Monitor in my palm out to her. "I found the broadcast, and they mentioned Bridget Klein."

Emi gasped. "That's her, Adam." Her fear turned to joy. "That's my sister."

"I heard her boyfriend on the broadcast. They're outside Cincinnati."

Emi's expression deadened somewhat. "There are a million places outside the city."

"It's better than not knowing," I offered. "We'll figure out a way to get to them."

A tear rolled down her cheek, and she smiled. "I can't believe she's alive. I thought I lost her forever. Like . . . like Peter."

I hugged her. "There's something else I need to tell you. Your sister's boyfriend, I know him."

"What?" Emi had repositioned herself on the edge of the bed, her body raised ever so slightly off its surface. She was ready to run at any moment. Ready to find her family. "How do you know Ian?"

Ian. So that was who he became after he left Vegas. "I recognized his voice," I explained. "His name isn't Ian. At least I never knew him as that. He's *Aaron.*"

Emi cocked her head in confusion. "But," she began, then stopped herself to think. "You might be right," she said after a moment. "He told us he grew up in Vegas, but he never talks about his past. He said there were some things that should be forgotten."

I had to stop myself from clenching my fists. That made me angry. How could he have chosen to forget everything about Vegas? I'd been a part of that past. I'd been his friend.

But I was wrong to assume that Aaron had left because he chose to, not because he had to.

"Emi, what else can you tell me about A—"

"Shhh!" Eve whisper-yelled, grabbing Emi and me by our shirts and pulling us to the floor.

"What the fuck?" But she didn't have to answer me. A bright stream of light came pouring through the window blinds, projecting a grey and yellow pattern on the walls and bed above us.

"They don't know we're up here, do they?" Emi asked worriedly. I could feel her body shaking.

"I don't think so," Eve responded. "I'm sorry. I didn't mean to scare you. They shouldn't be able to see us through the blinds, but I wanted to make sure."

They shouldn't be able to see us, but it was possible. Infrared cameras were generally only used by Officers and military personnel to uncover people who committed heinous crimes, one of which was murder. The very thing for which I was wanted. They could have access to the technology.

My body was pressed against the floor, my rapid breath hot against the wood, my heart pounding in my chest, and my head spinning in suspense. They knew. They had to. There was no other reason they shown the light directly in our room. They'd seen something. I was sure of it.

All of a sudden, the door to the room creaked open. Every hair on my body stood on end, and I swore I couldn't breathe. This was it.

"Eve," Aimee whispered, and I automatically sighed a breath of relief. "Adam? Emi? Are you guys here?" She pushed her hair out of her eyes and squinted, trying to find us in the darkness.

I exhaled. "Down here." My breathing returned to

normal, but my heart wouldn't stop pounding, and my headache that had just been dull pressure in my forehead was growing steadily stronger.

"Come on," Aimee urged, her words coming out in a rush. "We're going to leave out the backdoor. Miles has the car waiting a few streets down. The two people moved on to the next house; we already made sure. There was no one else with them. We just need to give them a few minutes to get far enough away. Then we have to go. We can't wait any longer. We can't risk it."

"I don't get it," I muttered weakly. I didn't understand why they just left. They had to know that we were here. But my thoughts kept getting interrupted by the sharp pains in my temple. I dug my fingers into my scalp as if that would release the tension, but moving my arm that quickly only made my head swim.

I shook my head, trying to steady my vision, but it only made it worse. My head throbbed, and I groaned. I'd been fine only moments ago. There was a dull headache, but nothing like this.

"Adam, did you hear what Aimee said? We're going to head closer to Cincinnati, just long enough for me to get a strong enough signal to tap into the seismic radar." Eve said.

"We're leaving, Adam," Emi added. She sounded so relieved. "We're going to help Aimee, and we're going to find my sister."

I wanted to smile and hug her, but I couldn't bring myself up from my position on the floor. I squeezed my eyes shut after opening them for a second. It hurt to have them open, even in the darkness, and stars were beginning to form in my vision. *Not again.*

"Adam?" The worry came rushing back to Emi's voice. "What's wrong?"

Eve was like lightning. I felt her grab my hand to check my pulse. Then she lowered her ear to my mouth to listen for my breathing. I groaned again.

"Tell me what's wrong," she demanded.

"It's my . . . my . . . m—head."

She lifted my head into her lap. She was only trying to help, but it made it that much worse to move, and the floor had been cool, which helped more than I realized. "When was the last time you drank anything?" Her voice was nervous. "Adam, do you hear me?" I did, but her voice sounded like an echo.

"Adam?" Emi's voice was the last thing I heard before the pain in my head overpowered me and I passed out.

CHAPTER 15

"Mom, why are we walking?" I'd whined. "Everyone else is on the Tram or inside already." I'd accidentally stepped into a puddle, soaking my socks and shoes, and a sour expression crossed my face. There would be no going back to our apartment to change. I only had one pair of shoes. "Mom, my feet," I whined again.

She laughed lightly and picked me up, swinging me in a circle then setting me back down gently. She squatted in front of me and moved to zip up my raincoat. "When did you get so heavy?" she asked, smiling brightly.

My mother loved the rain. It was peaceful, she always said. It drowned out the overbearing crush of the Screens and life in the city. You could hear yourself think, for once. I hated the rain, but she always took me for walks when it stormed. I realized later on just how much I loved the feeling of the cool droplets falling on my face.

"It's just water, Adam," she'd said as she stood and took my small hand in hers. When she'd straightened up, a gust of wind blew, and her perfume overcame my senses. She smelled like summer and winter all at once: a mixture of roses and cedar.

My mother's ash-blonde hair, the color that matched mine, fell in soft curls at her shoulders on a normal day when she went to work in the city as a data collector for far less money than she deserved. But that day, the rain ran through her hair and down her face, washing away the curls and unveiling her hair that was as straight as mine. The rain made her appear more natural and beautiful, if it was even possible.

A Tram full of people on the tracks above the street on which we walked was slowing down as it came to a stop at one of its entrances. People stared down at us on the pot-holed street from the large, seamless windows of the Tram like we were insane.

"Mom, people are staring. We're the only ones still outside."

She rolled her eyes and drug me forward. We had no planned direction when we took our walks in the rain; we just went where we felt like going. Sometimes we went to the park downtown and watched geese swim in the man-made pond; they enjoyed the weather as much, if not more than my mother. Other times, we walked around our dilapidated neighborhood, looking at and admiring graffiti on the old buildings, usually painted by Untouchables. Art was a practice that was forgotten by the majority of human beings and was something my mother was extremely passionate about. That being said, she'd never admit that she'd tagged walls and painted emotional portraits of strangers during her time in college when she wasn't studying to become a data manager; that would have made her "different," which would have made us both outcasts. She did admit to me once, though, that she knew a group of Untouchables, but she told me I'd have to formulate my own opinions of them when I was older, despite how much I begged her to tell me more about who they really were.

As we walked along the rain-soaked pavement, we decided to take a walk down to one of the more unsavory sections of the neighborhood, which was adjacent to ours. It was the middle of the day, so it was okay for us to go there, but it would get progressively worse as night approached. It would be nearly uninhabitable after nightfall.

Untouchables who disassociated themselves from the

academic values and overall views of the central group and had fully embraced criminal activity as a form of rebellion would harass, mug, and beat the shit out of anyone they could get their hands on, including children. Though I didn't see any of them while we walked deeper into the area, I felt like there were eyes always watching in the alleyways, behind dumpsters and piles of trash, just waiting for the right moment to make their move.

My grip tightened around my mother's hand as two teenagers ran across the street, laughing maniacally.

"Mom," I started in a hushed voice. "I don't want to be here."

"We're safe right now, honey, I promise. There is an understanding between them and people like us. Sometimes our beliefs align."

I didn't know what that meant, and it terrified me. My mother looked over in my direction. She saw the tears swelling in my eyes and quickly scooped me up into her arms, then rushed forward, stepping with a slight jump over a puddle of muddy-brown water on the street directly under another Tram overpass.

"One more block, Adam. We'll be back home before you know it."

A shiver ran down my spine. The rain chilled me, but it wasn't because of that. My mother, who loved the rain, had quickly gone from happy and smiling to looking around anxiously and pressing me so tightly to her chest, I thought I might break. Her heart beat so fast, I could feel her pulse where my arm was around her neck as she held me. Something was not right.

We turned a corner at the next block and headed down a narrow street with cracking concrete buildings and those with bricks falling out onto the street. It was a double row of residential housing that had long since been foreclosed on.

Suddenly, my mother stopped in front of a brick building that was divided into multiple apartments. There was so much dirt accumulated on the façade; much of the brick that would be bright red on a new building was a faded brown rust color. That, or nearly black with algae.

The windows on the second floor of the building were busted out, and boards covered those on the first floor facing the street. "You're mine" was sprayed in sloppy black letters on one of the boards and over onto the cracking brick and mortar. My mother held me closer to her chest. Her heart pounded under my palm, and I dug my fingers into her sweater. I was no longer interested in where we were going or why. I just wanted to be back in our two-room apartment with our tattered bedding lying over a mattress on the ground, and the overly worn leather couch that was ripping at the seams in multiple places. For all its lack of grace, at least our apartment was home. We were so far from home.

"Mommm?" I drew her name out. My voice sounded so small compared to the sound of the rain pounding against the roofs and street. "What are we doing here?"

Tears swelled in my mother's eyes, but she quickly blinked them back. "Don't be scared, baby. You'll be okay. I promise you'll be okay." But I was scared. My mother wasn't easily frightened. I knew something was wrong.

She walked closer to the house off the sidewalk and onto the concrete steps, skipping the lower one that crumbled onto the broken concrete of the sidewalk below, warped from the massive tree roots underneath.

I wanted more than anything in that moment to bury my head in my mother's chest, to breathe in her smell of roses, to have her sing to me and tell me things about the world that I never learned in school. I wanted to forget about where we were, but I couldn't tear my eyes away from the wood door in front of us with peeling red paint.

My mother lifted her fist and knocked lightly. For a minute, we stood side by side and nothing happened. Then, out of nowhere, I heard several locks unhitching, and the door slowly opened, creaking ever so slightly.

"Quick, get in," a man said in a low voice riddled with anxiety.

My mother slipped through the door swiftly with me in her arms, and it immediately shut behind us, thudding softly. I peered over my mother's shoulder as the man clicked all three locks back into place, but he was concealed by shadows. He took a step forward into the light, and I didn't expect what I saw.

He wore large, rounded frames around his eyes, unlike most people who opted for corrective eye surgery. Instead of taking away from his features, the glasses made him more distinctive and highlighted his hazel-green eyes that stood out from his pale complexion. Equally distinct was his dark brown hair that appeared jet black when compared to his porcelain skin. He must have been in his forties, as he had grey wings along the sides of his hairline. Again, it fascinated me because I wasn't used to seeing natural age in that way. Even when the man didn't have his eyebrows creased in worry or concentration, there was a sharp line between his brow, along with other age lines forming on his temple and around his mouth.

As my mother and I entered the crumbling building, the man turned immediately from the door to peer through a hairline crack in one of the wood panels acting as a windowpane.

"I'm sorry it took me a minute to answer," he said while he watched outside. "I didn't want to leave you exposed out there, but you can never be too certain who is watching." He finished and finally looked at us. My mother had set me down at that point, though my hand was still firmly grasping hers, and right as the man saw my mother, he pulled her into a hug.

"Are you okay, Sal?" he asked gently, still holding onto her. My mother's name was Salone. No one ever called her "Sal."

"Tony" was all she could manage to say before she started to cry. Her body shook as the man held her, trying to talk to her calmly and soothe her.

"Please tell me I'm making the right decision." My mother cried, falling away from his embrace. Her eyes met mine, and my lower lip began to tremble. I hated seeing her upset more than anything. It broke me on the inside.

She tried to smile, but it wasn't genuine. She couldn't hide how she was feeling from me. It pained me even more because I never saw her that way. I always wondered how she hid her emotions for so long, trying to protect me.

The man knelt down before me, and his eyes watched me closely from behind the frames. I wasn't afraid of him any longer. There was something about him that was inviting and friendly. Maybe it was his eyes that seemed to smile even when he wasn't.

"How do you feel?" he finally asked. I felt calm, but I knew it wasn't my own emotions that produced the feeling. My Monitor had stabilized them, but there remained a twisting feeling in the pit of my stomach that told me what I was feeling wasn't my own. Despite that, I mumbled "okay."

"You're going to be able to feel much more than okay soon, Adam," Tony said. "You'll be able to think clearer, you'll see the world for what it truly is—good and bad—and you'll be able to decide for yourself just who it is you are." He glanced between us, then directed my mother. "You're doing the right thing, Sal. I promise he'll be okay. Better than okay." He turned back to me. "And you're strong, aren't you, Adam?"

I'd never seen myself as strong, but in that moment, that was exactly what I'd wanted to be. For my mother, above all else.

I strained my ears to try to listen to the rest of their conversation, but their voices grew muffled and started to fade. I tried to hold onto the picture of my mother, tried to reach out for her, but she was getting farther and farther away from me.

I was somewhere between being asleep and awake, but I didn't fully realize where I was or what had happened before I started dreaming. All I knew was that my head was killing me and that I still wanted to be with my mother. I tried to imagine the smell of roses; it had seemed so real only moments ago, but it was gone. I didn't realize how much I'd missed that smell. I'd avoided roses for years after her death. It was too painful to be reminded of how someone who loved life once could kill herself. She did it to protect me; I fully believed that, yet I couldn't imagine having the strength to pull the trigger.

I felt sick to my stomach. I didn't want to think about that day because it was one of the reasons that lead to her death. It was the day my Monitor was destroyed. Tony was a doctor—one who performed *the* surgery—and had known my mother since they were kids and even knew my father, though I never had the chance to ask him about the man. I only ever saw Tony one more time after the surgery, but my splitting headache and the sleep-inducing drugs being pumped through my veins made the last memory of him a haze. I never saw him again after that because he was killed. My mother had been right to be afraid. Someone *had* been watching us the day she took me to his house. Someone had turned him in, and the authorities didn't waste time capturing the criminal that gave me my life back, though I did nothing of note with it until I broke out of the Border.

A few months after Tony was arrested, the Officers came for my mother. I was aware and had recovered enough from the surgery to know what was happening when they did, and I was aware enough to escape and run when she told me to. I left the part of the city where I grew up with her and was on my own for several weeks in another district of Vegas until an Officer found me. His name was Nick.

He fed me, gave me new clothes and a place to sleep. He didn't turn me in, though he had every incentive to. But he didn't. He kept me hidden and taught me how to hide who I really was and what had happened to me. He overwrote my personal information stored on my identification chip, erasing the old Adam and giving me a new history. After a while, the people searching for me forgot my face, and I moved on to an orphanage downtown. He would've kept me if his colleagues hadn't started to get suspicious.

That was how I ended up where I was and how I eventually met Aaron.

. . .

People were speaking, but their voices were like distant echoes, and I couldn't exactly make out what they said. I was swimming in the darkness behind my closed eyes, trying desperately to make the images of Tony and my mother reappear. I hadn't thought about that day in so long. It was painful to think about how afraid my mother was, but the memory was one of the last that I had of her. I wanted to hold onto it and never let it go. More than that, I wanted to hold onto everyone in my life who'd left it so abruptly: Tony, my mother, Nick, Aaron, and Linda. But they were gone.

Just breathe, Adam, just breathe.

The autonome went over a pothole in the street, jostling my body violently. It was then that the images of the people I loved fell away and the voices around me became discernible. My eyes fluttered open to see Eve, my head resting on her lap, and Emi, whose hand held tightly onto mine as she spoke with Eve.

The inside of the autonome was identical to the one we arrived at the suburb in, and it took me a minute to realize that we'd made it. We'd left the home and found the autonome that Miles's sister sent. Rather, they'd accomplished all that. The last thing I remembered was lying on my back in the room, heaving before I blacked out. Eve had asked me if I'd drank anything recently. I hadn't. I'd been so worried about Emi and Eve that I didn't realize my own body needed to be taken care of. I'd blacked out from dehydration. If I had the energy, I'd laugh at my own ignorance.

"Do you think it's possible Adam knows Ian?"

"I don't know, Emi. You said Ian never really talks about his childhood, so I think it could be possible."

"*Aaron,*" Emi let the name roll off her tongue, turning it over in her mind. "It suits him better."

"Just be careful," Eve warned. "He probably had a good reason to hide who he really is."

"Like Adam?"

I shut my eyes just before Emi looked down at me. "Tell me what happened, Ara."

"The security agent was going to kill him. I couldn't let that happen. Adam is a good person. He would never hurt someone if it weren't a life-threatening situation."

I was going to open my eyes and ask them where we were going, but the medicine Cal had presumably given me pulled me back into a lull, and I couldn't focus on their conversation. My attention drifted to the low hum of the autonome's engine. It wasn't long before I was asleep once more.

My body rocked back and forth.

"Adam?" Emi laughed softly. Then I felt her breath on my ear. "You're going to miss dinner if you keep sleeping." She sighed, then pushed me again. "Wake up."

When I opened my eyes, I winced and immediately closed them again. I had to blink a few times to adjust myself to the bright afternoon light. Once I could finally see, Emi's face appeared before me. She was beaming as she sat cross-legged next to me, her blue-grey eyes twinkling and her dimples set deep in her light brown skin. It was almost as if her freckles were dancing across her face with the movement of the sunlight shining through the canvas tent over us that rippled in the wind.

"You're looking much better," she said cheerfully. "You should've seen yourself after you passed out. All pale and purple. Like the life had been sucked out of you. Promise you'll take better care of yourself?"

I smiled weakly, still groggy from the medication I guessed Cal gave me. "Did Cal—"

"Yes," Emi cut me off, then grimaced. "He put a tube down your throat to get fluids in you once we made it to the autonome." She grinned slightly. "Miles was complaining about how heavy you were the whole time." She laughed again and handed me a glass of water.

I pushed myself up on one elbow. The throbbing headache

and nausea were gone, but I still felt off.

I glanced around while I took a sip of the cool liquid. I was lying on a doubled-up blanket on a patch of grass under the makeshift canvas tent held up by sticks. I wore only my underwear, and the agent's black helmet lay at my feet.

"If you're wondering where your clothes are," Emi started, "my sister insisted they needed to be washed. In her defense, Miles's blood was still all over them."

"Tell her I said thank you." I was uncomfortable without the uniform on, but I had a bigger concern. Where were we? "Emi, where did we end up?"

"Just outside the city. Maybe 7 miles. Spencer, Kena, my sister, and Ian have a small camp set up. It's great, really. There's a small river not far away, and don't worry, we're not out in the open. We're surrounded by woods for as far as you can see."

"Woods?"

"Mt. Airy forest outside Cincinnati. It's still one of the biggest parks near the city, and it's pretty well kept, all things considered. There's a lot of trash around, but it's better than nothing. We haven't run into any people yet. Nearly everyone has left the city and surrounding areas for the northern cities, or Anchorage, if they can afford it—oh! I also found some wild plants to eat, along with the canned food and granola bars Spencer and Kena have. But that will only last so long. I used to love hunting for berries around the farm." Her face fell in recollection.

I tried to process what she said, still dazed. We'd all been through so much, but we were alive. This camp sounded like exactly what we needed. It sounded safe. "Is everyone okay?" I asked, my mind drifting back to Eve as it usually did, then it hit me. Emi mentioned her sister!

I was suddenly sitting upright. "Emi!" I grabbed her shoulders enthusiastically. "We found your sister? How?" I had so many questions. Only a couple hours had gone by, but I'd missed so much.

Emi smiled widely, clearly enjoying my unexpected

cheerful state. "Everyone is fine. Ara managed to track Spencer and the group using the GPS system in the new autonome. They were well hidden, but the amount of signals used to broadcast their talk show is what gave them away. It was smart of her, but now that we know we can be discovered, we're going to have to move." She frowned. "That's why you need to eat and get your strength back." Seeing my disappointment, she added, "We can't stay in any one spot for too long. It isn't safe."

I knew it wasn't, and I knew we'd have to leave eventually if we were going to help Untouchables get out of Cincinnati, but it depressed me all the same. This seemed like it would be a good base, from what she described.

I smiled at Emi and thanked her. "I'll try to eat." It wasn't what I wanted to do. I wanted to meet her sister and, more than that, I wanted to meet Ian. I *had* to. I had to know if Aaron was alive. Food would come second to that.

"Good," Emi responded. "Now get your butt up!" She shoved my shoulders playfully, then jumped to her feet and turned to go out the flap that served as a door in and out of the tent, but she stopped right before she did. "Oh, Adam?"

"Yeah?"

"You were right. Don't tell the others, but you were right." Her playful smile was gone, replaced by a serious expression that hardened her face.

"Right?"

"About Aaron," she whispered in a low voice before leaving the tent.

An anxious feeling erupted in the pit of my stomach. *Great.* I had been right. Where did that leave me? With 11 years of catching up with someone I no longer knew. With someone who left without a word when I was twelve. So much had happened since then, yet so little compared to what I imagined to be the eventful life Aaron led after Vegas. I wanted to know, but how could I ask him? We weren't kids anymore, and we weren't friends. We were strangers.

My body fell back on the scratchy quilt, and I sighed

loudly. *Just think about Emi. She's okay. She found Bridget.*

The flap opened again, startling me, and I expected to hear Emi's annoyed voice telling me to move faster, but it wasn't her. A man a year or two older than me stood at the entrance just inside the tent. He didn't smile, but he didn't frown either. He was watching me.

His blonde hair was shorter than the way he wore it when we were young, and there was a shadow across his jawline from a lack of shaving that the Aaron I knew never had. Although he'd grown into a twenty-something adult, his blue eyes were still as bright and inviting as when he was thirteen.

While I looked at him, I unknowingly lifted my hand to feel my own stubble on my face. How could we still be friends? We got along so well once, but that was 11 years ago.

Aaron noticed me touch my face and the corners of his mouth twitched into a smile. "Never thought we'd make it into our twenties then, did we? Sixteen always seemed like the end-all."

The anxious feeling that turned my stomach subsided, and I couldn't help but laugh. "Did you ever get around to hijacking an autonome to celebrate your sixteenth?"

He laughed along. "Nope. Just got drunk and threw empty beer bottles at a Tram."

"We did that when we were twelve."

"Old habits die hard." He chuckled.

My face fell. "I bet you didn't expect to meet me like this." I sighed. "I'm a fucking mess, aren't I?"

Aaron's expression became serious again. "The world is a mess."

We looked at one another more closely, trying to find our former selves and reliving old memories. Aaron used to tell me all the time that the world was a mess. He went between seeing it for how beautiful it could be, like Emi, to being the pessimistic cynic I generally was.

Aaron finally looked away, as if it hurt to think about the past, then held out the black security agent's uniform to me. "Never thought you'd be wearing one of these."

I shook away the memories and drew myself back to the present and the stark realization of who I'd become. "Didn't you hear? I'm wanted for murdering the man who actually wore it."

"I'm so sorry, Adam."

I stood and took the uniform from his hands, then pulled it on as quickly as I could. "It beats working at a bar in Vegas, wondering when it will be my turn to face the end." I shook my head. "Sorry. Things have just been, well, absolutely fucked. I'm just glad I could help Emi. She reminds me of you."

His expression lightened at the mention of her. "She's a good kid. Bridget and I were worried sick." He touched my shoulder. "Thank you, Adam."

"I can't believe you're going to be a father," I said, remembering Bridget was pregnant. "Are we really that old?"

Aaron dropped his hand and laughed again. "No, I—" He paused, lost in thought. "We, Bridget and I, didn't plan to have a kid, but I'm glad it happened. I've always wanted a daughter."

"I didn't know that," I muttered, and he frowned.

"I wish I could go back and change the way things happened; I really do. But I had to leave Vegas."

I wasn't going to ask him about it. We'd only just met again. I wanted to know what happened, but it was also painful to remember how lost I felt without him for the first year or two after he left. I was alone, again. "You could've told me at least."

"Will you two hurry up?" Eve called from outside the tent. "Emi is going to flip out if you don't get out here soon."

"Aar—"

"Call me Ian. It's okay if Emi and Ara know, but I don't trust the others, okay?"

Right. Erase the past. My resolution to wait to ask what happened flew out the window. "*Ian*, what do you mean you had to leave?"

"You could have died."

My eyes widened in surprise. Who would want to kill a twelve-year-old? Something must have happened. Aaron must have been in trouble. "What do you mean I could've died?"

"I'll tell you later," he said in a rush. "Right now, we need to eat. We have to get out of here before someone finds us like your group did."

The last thing I wanted to do was eat. I was no closer to understanding why he left, and the fact that he did because my life was in danger felt like something that needed immediate explanation under normal circumstances. Unfortunately for us, life was no longer normal.

We finished dinner—a quick meal of canned corn and loafed bread next to a fire—and my head was still whirling from my conversation with Aaron. Like so many of us, there were parts of Aaron's past that I didn't know. I could never hold that against him, but there was one fact about his vague response to why he left Vegas that took root in my mind and was spreading like a virus, consuming my every thought. He left because he had to. He left because I could've died.

Theories formed in my mind. Maybe there had been a radical that was part of the group of Untouchables he belonged to at the time. If that person found out I wasn't one of them, that I could sell information about the group to the authorities, then maybe that would've made me too much of a liability. But wouldn't Aaron leaving make it all the easier to track me down and get rid of me? Maybe they gave him an ultimatum. Leave and never speak to the outsider again, and we won't kill him. It seemed like the only plausible explanation to me, but then again, the Aaron I knew could be very different from the Aaron his group did.

"You're so quiet," Eve murmured. We were alone under the canvas tent. Emi, her sister, and Aaron were in another setup near ours, while Cal and Miles were still speaking with Spencer and Kena, the two broadcasters who were originally from Cincinnati, outside by the fire. Avery was confined to his own tent.

I asked Eve if she believed he was the one who'd alerted Defense and Security we were in the suburb. I still wasn't convinced the security agent and blonde woman we'd seen were even part of a search for us. If they'd been looking for murderers—me and Eve—they would've used infrared technology to see into the homes to know for certain if anyone was there. They hadn't done that. Either they were absolute amateurs, or they were a search and rescue team like Avery, Cal, and Miles were.

I lay on my back on the quilt, staring at the pointed ceiling of the tent, while Eve sat across from me with her head in her hands, thinking about what I'd asked. We had an hour or two before the group left the site in Mt. Airy, headed closer to the city. Who knew how long we had here until someone found us or the earthquakes continued. Aimee hadn't had access to the seismic monitor in over a day.

"I don't think he did it," Eve said after a moment. Her dark hair was slicked back and still dripping wet. Emi's sister had insisted we all rinse ourselves off in the river along with our clothes. I had to admit that it felt nice to be immersed in the cold water, even if only for a few minutes.

Eve gathered her dripping hair in her hands and rung it out on the grass floor next to her. "What about you? Do you think he did?"

Avery was the main reason the three agents had offered to help Eve, Aimee, and me, making the final decision to reset the coordinates of the autonome away from Vegas and to Detroit after we'd left the outpost. But when he'd agreed that we should get to Cincinnati and help people at the epicenter of all this, he hadn't known who Eve and I really were or what we'd done. I didn't have access to the images the media portrayed on the Monitors of what happened, but I could only imagine. They probably showed a picture of the lifeless agent with the hole in the back of his head, spinning some story of how he was a hero trying to detain the terrorists that caused the outbreak at the Border. I knew an agent that was a hero once, and the man that killed Linda and tried to kill me was nothing like him. Nothing like Nick. I'd thought of him like a father for the year that I was with him, and I wished he was here in the tent to give me advice. He always had a way of calming me down and helping me realize things weren't as devastating and life-altering as I sometimes made them out to be. That was when I was in middle school and a kid making fun and calling me an Untouchable felt like the end of the world. That was before people were debating whether or not we were living through Judgement Day on the radio.

"I think Avery was just scared," I said finally. "He just wanted to be home with his husband."

Eve nodded and looked me directly in the eyes. My heartbeat quickened with her gaze on me, and I lifted myself up from my position on the ground to see her better.

"I wish I would have met you before I lost my job," she said. "Before everything went to shit."

I knew she was being serious, but it made me grin. "You wouldn't have liked me. If you wouldn't have had that dream, you wouldn't have taken any notice of the drunk college dropout at the bar. You would've found me extremely annoying and way too cynical to be around."

That made her smile, which made my heart skip a beat. "I already do," she said with a small laugh, then continued, "but you're also compassionate. You gave people hope at the bar. You gave them advice that saved their lives. That, and your terrible taste in music made them momentarily forget about their problems."

I rolled my eyes, and she kicked me softly with her leg. "Most importantly, you make Emi happy. You make her smile." She blushed, grinning to herself. "You make me smile. I wouldn't change a thing about you. I just wish you'd known me before I became Ara."

I moved closer to her and cupped her face gently in my hands. "It doesn't matter who you were or who you became. All that matters is who you are now, *Eve.*" It felt good to say her real name aloud. It felt right. Like a promise. Like no matter who we were to anyone else—Ara, Hanson—it didn't matter. We'd be true to one another.

"*Adam,*" she breathed softly.

My lips crashed into hers, and everything fell away. The only thing that mattered was her.

I stared into the darkness, trying to fall asleep and thinking about how good it felt to be next to Eve. It didn't matter how we were brought together—if there was an explanation, if it was just coincidence, or something else entirely—all I wanted was to be with her, and I hoped that after this was over, we could do a lot more than take Miles up on his offer to help get our identities changed. I hoped to leave the life we'd led before, to become a part of the Untouchables if we could, and I hoped Emi would be there with us. I was suspicious of Aaron, but Emi and her sister were kind and incredibly intelligent. They also knew how to live off the land and survive without the help of the Regime—knowledge we desperately needed if we planned to leave the society that had trapped us for too long.

Imagining what life could be like still didn't completely erase the churning sensation that I hadn't been able to get rid of since we broke through the Border in Vegas. Apart from the possibility of getting caught once we got into Cincinnati, I didn't know what was going to happen with the disasters, and that scared me to death. How were any of us going to make it out of this? What if the Dome, or the Regime itself, didn't exist after everything was over?

I wanted to turn my brain off. I hated thinking about our chances and how slim they seemed, but I couldn't help it, and eventually, my thoughts drifted back to my mother. Maybe she was right to take the easy way out . . . What was wrong with me? What she did wasn't the easy way out. I couldn't imagine how difficult it would be to leave the one thing in the world you loved the most—for her, that was me—because you had to.

I rolled over on my side and tried hard to think about

something, anything positive, but nothing would come. Instead, I fell asleep replaying the day my mother had raced through the streets toward Tony's, holding me tightly to her chest, trying to hide from me how terrified she'd been, and the uneasy look on his face as he'd held her and told her it would all be okay.

My mother's voice echoed through the air close by. She sounded worried.

I rubbed my eyes, feeling like I was in a thick fog. My head was aching, the dull pain radiating from a spot on the back left side of my head. I reached up to feel it and immediately wished I hadn't. My hair was buzzed in a rough patch around an inch-long set of stitches. I could feel the dried blood around the sutures that still oozed in places. My stomach turned, and I gagged. The sudden movement caused a sharp pain to blur my vision, and I whined pathetically.

The room was completely dark in an attempt to keep as much external stimuli from making the headache any worse.

"How long until he can leave?" I heard my mother ask.

"The longer you wait, the better," Tony's firm yet sympathetic voice replied. "He needs to be here for at least the next few days until the headaches let up. I need to make sure he's attached to the IV as well. I trust you could do it, Sal, but I want to make sure. He's a good kid, and he deserves this life."

"I wish we could have led ours without the Monitors. Can you imagine?"

"I do. All the time. But the procedure to remove them is much more complicated on adults; you know that. We risk losing our lives. The younger the person, the more willing the brain is to function without it. The longer you wait—"

"The longer you need it," my mother finished Tony's sentence.

"I always envied Isaac for that reason." My mother went quiet, and Tony apologized. "I shouldn't have brought him up. I'm sorry."

"It's okay—" She stopped herself. "No, it's not. But he had

a good reason to leave, and he wouldn't have if I hadn't made him."

"Do you ever see him?" Tony asked cautiously. "I always expect him to be right around the corner, waiting to take us on our next great adventure. I regret a lot of things, but meeting him is not one of them. I wouldn't be doing this procedure if I hadn't. He made me realize risking my life to give others freedom is always worth it."

I heard my mother sniffle and begin to cry. "I miss him. Part of me wants Adam to know him now. Part of me wants him to make that decision on his own in the future."

"There are good and bad sides to being a part of that world, same as being a part of everyday society. The system may be flawed, but there are reasons we chose to remain a part of it."

"Besides the fact that we're stuck with our Monitors?" Salone asked, laughing a little. Tony laughed with her, and I couldn't help but imagine what they'd be like together. Tony seemed like a good man, someone my mother deserved.

"Do you think he'll be okay? I mean, really okay? It's going to be hard trying to blend in."

"Yes," Tony agreed. "But on the inside, his thoughts will be his own, and that is the most powerful thing in the world."

My mother laughed again. This time, she sounded happier. "That's what Isaac used to say."

"And he was right." There was another moment of silence while they listened to my labored breathing. My head was foggy, and my body begged me to give in to sleep, but I kept fighting to stay awake. My mother never spoke of my father, Isaac.

"I've seen the boy around," Tony began again. "He seems kind but far too fearless."

"It will get him into trouble one day, like Isaac. He needs to be careful," Salone said worriedly.

"Given the situation he came from, I'd say he's doing pretty good."

"He's Isaac's adopted son. I'm just worried about him.

Isaac is a great leader, but I don't know if he can be a father."

"Aaron will be okay, Sal. Maybe one day he and Adam will cross paths."

I jolted awake, panting heavily. *Aaron? Aaron knew my father?*

"No fucking way," I muttered under my breath, casting a quick glance at Eve to make sure I hadn't woken her up. She was sound asleep next to me.

The dream felt so real. Was it a memory? When I tried to think back to that time before I lost my mother and Tony, all I remembered was the feeling of numbness and vague pain in the back of my head. Was it possible?

My father's name was Isaac Mathers.

My mother's name was Salone Locke.

My real name was Adam Locke, and the only thing I knew about my mother's past that related to the Untouchables was that she knew several from her time in college. My mother met my father in college, but she never *ever* spoke about him. The only thing I knew about him was his name. I always figured she would tell me more once I got older. I believed she would have if she'd lived to see me grow up.

Tony knew my father as well, but the man had been killed for his crimes against the Regime. There was no one else in my past I could ask. No one but Aaron. If my father was an Untouchable from a group in Vegas, like Aaron, it was plausible the two met. But Aaron as my father's adopted son? Was that why I'd seen him outside the abandoned building day after day until I gained the courage to introduce myself? Had he been waiting for me long before that?

"Maybe one day they'll cross paths." I turned Tony's words from my dream over and over in my mind, then thought about what Aaron had said earlier: *"I had to leave . . . You could have died."* Was there a reason my father had to stay away all those years? My mother said herself there was. Was whatever trouble Isaac was in enough to kill me and endanger Aaron?

I focused on controlling my breathing as I tried to figure it out. While I did, I finally took closer notice of Eve. Her body shifted constantly, and her face was screwed up in a mixture of pain and fear. She was sweating, and her dark hair stuck to her face. She was having a dream. No, a *nightmare.*

I reached a hand out to gently wake her, but before I could, a low rumble came from below us, and my heart stopped momentarily. *No.*

Again, a tremor shook the ground softly beneath us. It wasn't enough to wake anyone up but enough to be noticed by anyone who already was. I sat frozen under the canvas tent in the woods in Mt. Airy, waiting. For a minute, nothing happened and I thought I imagined it all, but then the ground shook for a third time, enough to rock Eve's body back and forth with aggression and cause her to wake up. The first thing she saw when she did was my expression of sheer horror.

"It's too late," I whispered, and her eyes widened with terror.

Suddenly a voice was yelling outside the tent, screaming orders. It was Aimee. "Get up! Get up! We're out of time! This could be bad, very bad. We need to get as far enough away from the city as possible!"

"We're sitting ducks if we stay," Eve said quickly, jumping up and out through the flap in the tent.

"Don't worry about the tents and other stuff! Just make sure we have everyone!" Aaron commanded, going between tents and making sure that everyone was at the campsite.

I was outside the tent in a flash. I stood, my fists clenched tightly, while everyone ran around the site. Spencer and Kena were trying to grab their bags of food and equipment. I could've helped them, and the others, get to our and Spencer's autonome, but I didn't. My anger surged, and I couldn't think straight. Before I knew it, I was on Aaron. It wasn't a smart choice, but I was out of time. I couldn't die not knowing who he was.

"Tell me how!" I screamed at the top of my lungs. "How do you know Issac?"

"Adam! What are you doing?" It was Emi. She could try all she wanted, but it was too late to stop me. All the anger and frustration that had built up from the moment I walked down the street on the way back to the orphanage and ended up waiting in an alley all night for my friend that would never show up came flooding out. He left without a trace, just like my father. In a moment, I had turned into Avery, and the worst part of it was that, unlike Miles, Aaron didn't fight back. That only made my anger all the more pointed.

I shoved Aaron to the ground and pinned him underneath my legs. "Tell me how you know my father!" My face was inches from his.

He watched me closely with his big blue eyes full of understanding and sadness.

The rage ate away at my insides, begging me to punch him and break his nose. I wanted to make him pay for keeping secrets.

I raised my hand to strike, ignoring Bridget, Emi, and Miles's screams to stop, then I remembered the way Emi looked at Avery when he attacked Miles. She looked at him like he was a monster. Had I turned into that monster because of a dream I didn't know was real?

"I'm sorry, Adam," Aaron said breathlessly, and I lowered my hand.

"Let her go!" Bridget screamed at Eve, who held Emi tightly in her arms to stop her from attacking me. Aaron was part of her family, her real family, and I had suddenly gone from someone who reminded her of her brother, someone she thought she could trust, to a threat.

"You know Adam would never hurt him!" Eve glanced at me, shaking her head. "Don't," she mouthed.

"Stop it!" Cal yelled at them.

Aimee had pulled Miles away. "They'll handle it! We have to get Avery and whatever supplies we can grab! We don't know how long we have!"

Spencer and Kena were already working on getting their broadcasting and other equipment in the autonome they'd been using since they'd found it abandoned outside the city.

The earth below us continued to tremble.

Emi broke free and was on me before I could move, shoving me to the ground. "You asshole! I trusted you!"

"Emi, stop!" Aaron yelled hurriedly. "Adam had every right to!"

Emi turned sharply and glared at him. "Every right? What are you talking about?"

Bridget ran over and tried to help Aaron up, but he stopped her. Eve was already at my side.

Emi looked at her, and tears started to form in the corners of her eyes. "What is happening?"

"Emi," Aaron said evenly, "I need you to help Bridget get to the car. I need to talk to Adam."

Emi didn't move. "I'm not a child. I can handle it." Yet, Aaron treated her like she wasn't strong enough to hear what he was going to say to me, just like I wasn't strong enough to hear it back when I was twelve.

"Just tell me," I said, staring at him. "I don't want to die not knowing the truth."

Aaron took a deep breath. Then his eyes fell to the ground. "Your father was in trouble. He was wanted for a so-called terrorist attack on one of the main signal towers in the city. He wanted to shut it down, just for one day. Just to give people an idea of what life could be like. The life you and I had access to." He looked up, shaking his head and wiping away tears. That, more than anything else he could've done, felt like a punch to my gut. He cared.

"Isaac raised me, but believe me, Adam, he talked about you all the time. You were his real son. It wasn't hard for me to track you down. I wanted to know about the boy he always spoke of. I wanted to know my . . . my brother."

Eve, Emi, and Bridget all gasped, completely speechless.

Miles had helped Avery into one of the autonomes and was walking over to help diffuse the situation. He stopped in his tracks when he heard Aaron's last sentence. "What the fuck?"

Aaron was right. It wasn't only a dream. It was a memory. My father hadn't been far away. He'd been near me my entire life.

"Why didn't you tell me?"

"The security team looking for your father knew about our entire group, which included me. If they figured out I was in contact with you, they would've quickly found out you didn't have a Monitor. Your whole past embedded in that identification chip would've been rendered a lie. They would've found out who your father was, and they would've killed you. I should've warned you, but the less you knew, the less the risk of you being discovered. I'm so sorry."

A tear rolled down my cheek, and I quickly wiped it away. Aaron wasn't lying.

"Wait, you two know one another?" Spencer asked, coming up beside us. "That explains the fight."

"If you don't all get up and get in the fucking autonomes, I will murder each and every one of you!" Aimee yelled from near one of the machines. "Let's go!"

Eve helped Emi up, and they started for the autonomes with the others. Miles hesitated before following, making sure I was going to be alright. I probably wasn't. None of us were. The fault zone was still active. If the tremors were still going on, I could no longer feel them, but that didn't mean they were gone. We'd been so naïve to think we had time. It was stupid of me to waste any of it, but I couldn't have died not knowing.

Aaron finally pulled himself from the ground and held out his hand to help me up. I took it, pulling him into a hug. "I resented you for so long," I started. "I hated you for leaving, but I was also worried you were dead. I can't believe I'm here with you now, at the end of the fucking world."

"I can't believe it either, but I'm happy. I should've come for you sooner. I didn't have to stay away." He didn't, but he did, just like my father. I finally understood why. Maybe I'd never know anything else about Isaac, but I'd know that he knew about me, and he cared.

"If it weren't for you," I told Aaron, "I wouldn't know how to live." I had wasted so much time feeling sorry for myself, drinking away my problems in bars until I started working for Linda, but that year I spent with Aaron by my side always affected me and always reminded me that there were people and ideas in life worth fighting for.

"Get in the machine now!" Avery bellowed from across the campsite where the autonomes were parked next to one another. The tape was off his mouth, and Miles stood next to him with a knife and the cut rope that had been around Avery's wrists in his hands. Miles had let him go.

Aaron and I exchanged one last glance before racing toward the open door on the autonome closest to him. As soon as we were in, the machine started up, its blue interior light casting an unearthly glow on everyone inside. Aimee, Miles, and Avery were in the front seat. Emi, Eve, and Bridget were in the middle row, and Aaron and I were behind them. Everyone's eyes were fixed on the dashboard where Aimee was tapping, pulling up different screens to read seismic energy. "I sent a signal to my colleagues back west to get access. I had to," she added quickly when Miles looked at her with astonishment. "This is bad. The readings were at an absolute zero earlier. I checked. For a moment, I thought I'd imagined the surge." I recalled all of us huddled in the suburban house, waiting to die.

The autonome was gaining speed, and the one with Cal, Spencer, and Kena was in front of ours. The trees blew past in a dark green and brown blur.

Avery shifted to turn and look at me. "I'm sorry I hurt you." I stopped him before he could say any more.

"I know. I believe you."

"I do, too," Miles said. "Cal is still on the fence, but you're our brother. If the world is really ending—"

"Don't say it," Avery said. "Don't even think it."

"Adam," Eve whispered, also turning around to look at me. "I'm . . ." She couldn't finish her sentence, and I noticed she was tapping her fingers nervously on her thigh.

"What is it?"

"Look at this!" Aimee exclaimed before Eve could respond, pointing to the area along the Cincinnati Arch Fault that caused the major energy surge days earlier and disappeared before any damage could be done. Gone without a trace, or so we thought. But there it was on the dashboard screen, and it wasn't alone. A point in the New Madrid Seismic Zone near Nashville was lighting up on her screen.

"Fuck," she cursed under her breath, then she yelled it again. "Fuck!" She punched the dashboard. "Ara, I have to send them another signal! You have to rewire my Monitor, just for a moment." Eve was staring at the floor of the autonome, her fingers continuously tapping. "Ara!" But she wasn't paying attention.

"I saw it," she mumbled. "It's just like the dream." She probably sounded crazy to everyone else, but I understood. It was *the* dream. Rather, *the* nightmare.

"Ara!" Aimee shouted again. "Adam, please help me!" But I couldn't get Eve's attention either.

"It's all happening like I saw it." She moaned. Her hands were shaking, and Emi tried to console her, but it didn't work. She didn't hear anything we said to her. It was like she was no longer with us but lost in the nightmare, continuously reliving it.

"I don't want you to die," she whispered, breathing in short gasps, but her eyes still didn't focus on me. "I don't want to die. It's—what they were talking about—Judgement—"

Everything I'd heard about it, the things I'd seen, raced through my mind: the paintings, with their swirling depths— what I now knew was called Hell—and demons eating their way through people, fire consuming them above and below, and the great cracks in the ground through which they fell; all the devastation around the coast and in the Capital; the dead little girl; the way Emi shivered and cried when she told us about the people who'd tried to kill her and her family; the earthquake in Cincinnati that started it all; and our dreams.

"Judgement," the old woman whispered. "He's watching us now."

"Who?" I asked. "Who's watching us? The guard?"

"No guard," she said. "He's watching," she repeated, pointing a shaky finger up toward the sky.

Eve was talking about the same thing the old woman at the

tracks had, the same thing Spencer and Kena debated about, and the same thing Emi, Bridget, and Ian almost died because of.

Emi looked at me, her expression sheer horror. She knew what Eve meant too.

But I never had the chance to tell her about the dream Eve and I both experienced. I never had the chance to tell her that it was crazy. This wasn't Judgement Day. There was no such thing. There was an explanation; there had to be. We just didn't understand. But I didn't even have time to react.

There was a huge tremor under the surface of the Earth, much bigger than the one Eve and I felt in the desert outside the Dome on the way to the outpost. For a moment, all I could hear was Emi's high-pitched scream, and then the world was turning and my stomach dropped.

It didn't hit me what had happened until I was lying on my left side in the overturned autonome. I must have passed out, but only for a few moments. The evening sun still shown through the trees, casting a golden glow over everything. I wanted to look out the window to my right to see if I could make anything out, but I was still too disoriented to fully realize we'd been in an accident. Water dripped down my forehead, further distracting me as I drifted between states of consciousness.

"It's an interesting debate. Interesting but terrifying, if not completely disturbing to those who don't believe in some form of God."

"I agree, Lita. We're talking about a being that is omnibenevolent and omnipotent, meaning that he, or whatever it is, is all good and all-powerful."

"Do you think someone who is wholly good could do this, May?" Lita asked. The two individuals had been asked to attend the broadcast hosted by their friends, Spencer and Kena.

"I don't. Not for a second. But that's just it. It's a matter of belief. Some people say that all of this is a test, that those of us that are truly faithful and repent for our sins will have a place in Heaven."

"But how could some wholly good being, more powerful than any other in existence, allow people to perish. And it's not just us, for that matter. What about the animals and the planet? How could this being not show us the way to save this world? He is that powerful, after all."

"It's an age-old argument. Let's take a look at several verses from Revelation. For those listening who are unaware of the book we are speaking of, it is called the Bible. It has long been forgotten by everyone except certain groups of Untouchables. There are fanatics among us who consider the enclosed words to be the absolute truth, though they don't see themselves as fanatics. We'll leave that decision up to you. Go ahead, Lita."

"I'm reading from Revelation 11:17-18. 'We give thanks to thee, Lord God Almighty, who art and who wast, that thou hast taken thy great power and begun to reign. The nations raged, but thy wrath came, and the time for the dead to be judged, for rewarding thy servants, the prophets and saints, and those who fear thy name, both small and great, for destroying the destroyers of the earth.'"

Lita finished, and May explained, "Human beings are considered the destroyers in this case. But how could this being not intervene? How could he let this happen in the first place? The Book of Revelation makes clear that the world was in need of a cleanse of human beings, but if we are to believe that we are going through Judgement Day as we speak, we need to realize that we aren't the only ones affected. Like I said, the entire planet is at stake: the flora and fauna? I guess some people believe it will right itself after some time and the only thing missing will be us. I just can't wrap my head around it."

"I think for many people, May, this goes back to the question of the test. Does the parent, God, intervene, or does he let his children make their own choices, whether good or bad, to save humanity?"

May scowled. "Jokes over! People are dying! Thousands of people, and they're not all bad! And let's not forget about all the children who have died! What child deserves a death like this, like we've seen projected in horrid detail on the Screens?"

"I agree. It kills me, but some people believe that if they are faithful, death is only a small part of a much longer journey. A long, long time ago, this way of thinking used to guide the majority of people's decisions. For some, it gave them a reason to live, to look past all of the bad in the world, and to focus on doing good and being better. At the end of life, of the 'journey,' they believed they'd meet this God, and thinking about how there was something good waiting for them after death gave them hope. For others, it was an excuse to do terrible things while they were living. Unspeakable things. They only needed to have faith and repent their sins, and all would be forgiven."

"Like murdering people and committing suicide in the name of God?" May asked angrily.

"It's terrifying and impossible for us to grasp, but to the radicals that attacked Bridget Klein's group—their own group—they weren't doing anything bad or evil. They were sacrificing themselves, and that sacrifice was for God in their hope of getting into Heaven. Others who believe might think that was the cowardly thing to do, to not face the supposed judgement, but it all goes back to what you believe in, and what you think is right based on that."

May took a deep breath, and the two women were silent for a moment until Lita started speaking again. "Listen to this. It's from John 3:16-17. 'For God so loved the world, that he gave his only begotten Son, that whosoever shall believe in him should not perish, but have everlasting life.'"

CHAPTER 16

The faint hum of a Monitor whirred, and the sounds of voices
gently drifted over me. The lull of their speech was more like
a slow fog wrapping itself around me. A drop of liquid pinged
against the glass where my head lay, and I watched its deep
red color expand and run into a hairline crack in the window
of the autonome. The voices kept on humming. They sounded
so far away, like I was listening to them from underwater. I
heard a loud sound like an explosion outside, but it was soft
and so distant, like the voices.

I hadn't fainted. I was aware, in ways, but it was like I was
swimming through a thick haze, and everything I tried to
focus on made me dizzy. My head must have hit the glass.
Hard.

I reached my hand up slowly to my forehead and felt a hot,
sticky liquid cover my fingertips. I could smell the iron as soon
as I brought my hand away. I was bleeding and suddenly
conscious of a stinging cut along my temple and cheek. Tiny
shards of broken glass from the windshield dug into my skin,
biting at my nerves.

The voices hummed again after a pause, continuing their
conversation, and my eyes focused on the Monitor lying in
front of my nose, its tiny black switch pushed to the "on"
position. It was the one Eve had given Emi in the suburb so
that she could listen for word about her sister. It was currently

tuned to Spencer and Kena's station. They must have set it to transmit their previous broadcast, a debate on the cause of the natural disasters.

My head was still extremely fuzzy and bright spots of light danced in my vision. All I could focus on was the object in front of me. The Monitor was a tiny device, smaller than the palm of my hand: a device that controlled nearly everyone's thoughts, including mine at one point. The earpiece that attached to it was generally made invisible by a medical implantation procedure, but it wasn't necessary.

I grabbed the tiny earpiece and weakly lifted it to my ear. The voice on the broadcast was reading. "I looked, and behold, there was a great earthquake; and the sun became black as sackcloth, the full moon became like blood, and the stars of the sky fell to the earth." She took a deep breath and continued. "Then the kings of the earth and the great men and the generals and the rich and the strong, and everyone, slave and free, hid in the caves and among the rock of the mountains, calling to the mountains and rocks, 'Fall on us and hide us from the face of him who is seated on the throne, and from the wrath of the Lamb; for the great day of their wrath has come, and who can stand before it?'"

"Fuck me," Miles groaned from the front seat, but my mind was far away from the safety of our group. What had I just heard on the broadcast? Was what the woman read part of the book Emi mentioned about the being—God?

Afraid, I tore out the earpiece and flung it toward the front of the autonome and out through the shattered windshield. What she read was deranged and completely irrational. It was fucking insane!

I screamed, and Miles moaned. "Shut up, Adam." He grunted. "Dammit, I think I broke my hand trying to stop myself from hitting the window."

"Is Aimee okay?" It was Avery's voice. His body was pressed under Miles's weight. I could see him through the break in the seats along the side of the autonome that was flipped on the ground, the side I lay on. He was in my same position. I immediately became aware of the heavy weight on my own side and how much my ribs hurt. A few were most likely broken.

"Aimee?" Eve asked, suddenly awake. Then she became frantic. Though I couldn't see her, I could hear the panic in her voice. "Aimee!" I could just make out her limp body over the top of the seats. She was slumped over Miles, and there was blood running down her face from the top of her head. There was so much blood. Too much. I glanced at the windshield and automatically knew what had happened. There was a spot of bloody glass on the right side where she'd been sitting.

"Avery . . ." Eve sounded like she could barely breathe. "Oh my god." Her voice broke, and she was sobbing hysterically. "Take her pulse!"

Eve had crawled onto the consul between the first and second rows of the autonome, and Bridget was in the second row lying on her back on the window I was on. Emi was right by her side, and they both kicked at the opposite window, trying to break it or kick the door open. "Harder!" Emi instructed.

I forced my eyes back open when they started to close. Their voices were all starting to sound like one loud siren echoing in my mind, and the pain in my side was growing. Aaron was too heavy. "A-Aaron." I coughed. "I need, I—" A sharp, stabbing sensation tore through my body, and I winced. "I need you to . . . to move."

Eve had gathered Aimee in her arms and was clinging to her body. "I can't feel a pulse. Avery, I can't feel anything!"

"Try harder, Bridget!"

"Miles, move!"

"I can't move! There's nowhere to go!"

I pressed my palm against the glass window and regretted it in an instant. The tiny shards scattered across the glass pierced my flesh, and I winced again but kept pushing myself up, though without much success. I got myself into a painful position on my back, trying to hold Aaron's body up with my legs. He wasn't awake and a sick feeling formed in the pit of my stomach. I had just found him. I couldn't lose him.

Bridget demanded Emi shield her face, and with one last blow, Bridget was able to kick out the broken window on the passenger door. Glass rained down on Emi's back, and she screamed, but none of it cut through her jacket.

"Come on!" Bridget yelled as she pulled herself through the window and out onto the ground outside. "Emi, come on!"

Emi quivered. There had to be a million individual shards of glass sticking out of her hair. She glanced at me as she crouched on the window next to mine, ready to stand and pull herself from the machine. Her eyes fell on Aaron and her face twisted in pain. "He's not . . ." She bit her lip, and her eyes started to water. I knew exactly what she was going to ask.

I thought about Avery's words from before, and I repeated them to her. "Don't say it. Don't even think it." Aaron couldn't be dead.

Emi hesitated, and I firmly told her to go. "Get somewhere safe. We'll be right behind you." I hoped we could, but Aaron was so heavy. Every time I tried to move or speak, I felt the stabbing pain in my ribs. We weren't going anywhere without help.

Eve was crying hard, and she screamed at Avery when he tried to make her move to get out. "No! I'm staying here with her. I can't leave her. She's going to wake up."

Avery left her alone and crawled over the seat around her and into the middle row. He scanned Aaron and me, then put his fingers to Aaron's neck to check for a pulse without a word. I held my breath as he did, and time seemed to slow down, to crawl, if only for a moment.

"He's alive," Avery said at last, exhaling audibly. He'd been holding his breath as well.

I sighed in relief and couldn't stop a tear from falling down my face. "You're alive," I whispered happily. "You're alive, you lucky bastard." He always seemed invincible when we were kids.

Avery left through the busted-out window, and Miles

followed shortly after. Then they both helped pull Aaron's unconscious body from the autonome and started carrying him away from the wreck. I forced myself to crawl over the seat and into the middle row, my broken ribs screaming in agony.

Eve's face turned toward me. I had never seen her look so upset. So utterly torn apart. "We're screwed, Adam," she muttered hopelessly. "We're fucking screwed." She held Aimee's head on her chest, but I couldn't bear to look at her bloody face. "She's, oh no. No, no, no. I can't believe it. It can't be true. I, she . . . she's dead." Eve closed her eyes and kept shaking her head. "I wanted to help save people. But now? We needed her."

A lump formed in my throat, and I couldn't help but imagine what would've happened if Aaron was in Aimee's place. But he wasn't, and Eve was right. The seismic readings made sense to Aimee. To us, they looked like a foreign language. We weren't geologists or seismologists. At least Eve was familiar with the field. I was just a bartender. I did know one thing, however. We had helped people. We helped Emi find her sister, and Eve helped me realize that life was about so much more than working at the bar. I wanted to believe the advice I gave people at the Back Door, but I never fully could. I had forgotten how to live, and it had started the day Aaron disappeared. My life had been one continuous screwup until the moment at the tracks when I met the old woman. Until the moment the world we knew began to end.

"What are you two still doing in here? We need to—" Spencer's voice broke through my thoughts, but she stopped as soon as she saw Eve. She peered at me, silently asking if Aimee was gone, and I nodded. Her face fell. "I'm so sorry, Ara, I really am, but we need to go. Our autonome, the one Cal, Kena, and I took, it blew up after we crashed. The earthquake caused us to flip." Her tone was uneasy, and I could see that her hands were trembling. "We have to hurry," she added in a rush. "The explosion started a fire. With how high the temperatures have been and the lack of rain, the whole forest could catch."

Eve looked at me with sad eyes. "I can't leave her."

"She's already gone."

The wind was so strong, and smoke seemed to fill every corner of the Earth. I heard coughing that confirmed Emi and Bridget were still walking behind us. We could run, but it was risky when we couldn't see where we were going. We could easily run into a tree or fall into water or off a cliff. It wasn't safe. The world had become grey and the evening sun that had burned brightly before was gone. All we could see was the orange fire behind us and the grey and black vapor all around us. I held Eve's hand firmly in mine, and we followed Cal, Miles, and Avery, who were all holding up Aaron. I could just make out the backs of their heads in the smog. Spencer and Kena were leading the way, and I couldn't see them whatsoever.

We started running at first until Bridget physically couldn't anymore from the baby. So, we slowed down and were trying to get as far away from the explosion as possible. If we didn't hurry, we could suffocate from the smoke, which seemed to be getting worse with the heavy wind and the growing size of the fire. Spencer had been right. The dryness had caused everything to catch almost immediately.

I thought about what happened before the accident and the way Eve had acted. The tragedy of Aimee's death had pulled Eve from her nightmare world, but she never explained what she meant. Had she known that was going to happen to us? That was too insane of a thought.

"What did you see?" I finally asked her.

She wrapped her other arm around mine and pulled herself closer to me. I winced when her arm brushed my ribs but didn't let it show. Her face was still red from crying, and her eyes were wet. "It was the same dream," she said. "The ground split in two, but instead of waking up before I saw you fall, I had to watch you die. It was horrible, and then Aimee . . ." Tears streamed down her face once more, breaking my heart again.

"I'm still here. I'm not going anywhere. I promise, *Eve*," I whispered her name. I no longer cared who we were surrounded by. It felt like a crime to continue to call her by a name that was created to erase who she really was.

I thought about Emi's reply when I told her I'd stay with her to make sure she lived to see her sister again. It was the promise that I wouldn't die. She told me not to make promises I couldn't keep.

I shook her words away. *Don't stop, Adam. You will stay alive. For Salone, for Linda, for Eve. Just don't stop.*

Eve doubled over, and I had to pick her up to keep going. She was suffering badly from the smoke inhalation. "It's going to be okay," I assured her. "We're going to make it through this." I thought about all the things we'd do if we did. "I'm going to take you on a real date, and we're going to go somewhere we can be safe and happy and away from all this. I'm going to make you fall in love with me, and we're going to watch Emi become an aunt and—"

Eve coughed again and stopped me, waving her hand. "I'm already in love with you. I was the moment I started watching you. When I saw who you really are. I love you so much." She wheezed after she finished. She was going to suffocate if we didn't hurry.

"I love you too. Now, stop talking. Save your oxygen."

I fell to my knees in the clearing. Eve clutched her sides, gasping in the fresh air as she collapsed in the grass beside me. The others were in various states of recovering from the asphyxiation, and we were drenched. It was pouring down rain, and I was cold, shivering before long. The thick smoke from the woods had burned my lungs, and the heat had been overwhelming. I turned my head from side to side to look at the wide-open space. We were surrounded by the woods, and it looked as though the fire was dying down from the heavy rain. Patches of mud were all over the grass, having formed from the intense shaking of the earthquake. I was petrified of putting in the earpiece again, not wanting to know what had happened at the epicenter or the one Aimee had shown us in the New Madrid Seismic Zone. But I did. I had to know if our world was dying. One way or another, I had to know.

I lay on my back, my lungs still burning from the smoke, while the rain came down in sheets all around me, soaking my uniform. Everyone was still panting hard, trying to catch their breath, but we were all here. Aimee wouldn't be forgotten, and I'd try as hard as I could to make sure everyone else survived. I watched Eve, breathing easier. She loved me. I never thought my life would turn out this way, but I had found the love of my life. I had found my family.

I took a final breath, preparing myself for what I was going to hear, and switched the Monitor to the "on" position. I searched for the broadcasts from the Capital, but all that came through was static. I kept searching until I heard a crackling noise, then a voice broke through.

"Is anyone still listening? My name is John. Does that even matter anymore? I just saw Mt. Spurr erupt . . . We had no idea it was coming . . . I can still hear their screams. How many people have to die?" The man was silent for a moment. "People used to say the Monitors were the death of humanity. I wonder if they still think that way. It doesn't matter. We'll all be dead soon. Then there won't be anyone around to disagree, to fight, or cause pain. We'll all be gone . . . finally equal." He choked up, and I could almost feel his body shaking from the tears over the broadcast.

"New Anchorage is no longer safe. It has been closed off because of the volcanic eruption. It's like the ash has turned daylight into darkness. They say that the lava will move slowly enough for people to escape, but where are we going to go? The Dome is failing, and sections of it are nonexistent. The eastern and northern pacific zones are flooding. There's no escaping it . . . and what can we do? Absolutely nothing. We're just waiting." He broke into tears again, unable to control himself. He no longer needed to. "We don't deserve to die! The actions of some shouldn't mean the death of all!

Humanity can't end . . ."

I pulled out the earpiece and let the Monitor fall next to me in the water running down the grassy hill that had become a mudslide. Aaron was lying, sprawled on the ground to my right. As I watched him, his eyes slowly fluttered open.

Eve coughed, bringing my attention to her. She spit out water as it ran down her face and into her mouth. "It's over," she said when she noticed I was looking at her.

"It can't be." I couldn't tell if the water streaming down her face was only from the rain or tears.

"I think this is the end."

I shook my head. "No. There's no such thing as an ending."

She closed her eyes.

She was wrong. She had to be. This was only the beginning for us. I wouldn't allow it to end this way . . .

Did I have a choice?

I closed my eyes against the rain and held tightly to her hand. I was cold, wet, and terrified, but there was a calmness to it all. It was strange yet peaceful, and though a small part of me wanted it to be the end, maybe it was just the beginning.

AFTERWORD

Although Adam and Eve are purely fictional characters living in a futuristic, dystopian world, the disasters that take place in this book and the commentaries that surface to try and explain them were inspired by Jan van Eyck and Rogier van der Weyden's *Last Judgement* paintings that Adam mentions learning about in middle school. While getting my undergraduate degrees in Art History and French, I chose to write a paper comparing Van Eyck (1390-1441) and Van der Weyden (1400-1464), both Netherlandish painters, and how their depictions of Judgement Day were heavily influenced by the Book of Revelation.

As an agnostic individual who grew up in a household where religion wasn't practiced, I hadn't been exposed in depth to the Bible and had no idea what the Book of Revelation (written c. 96 CE) was until one of my first art history courses. It was extremely fascinating and eye-opening to me to look at something from an objective viewpoint that was considered absolute truth for a huge percentage of the population for thousands of years. Art with a religious perspective spanned the Middle Ages to the Renaissance and well into the 19th and early 20th centuries, and religion was a cause of major conflict throughout that time. It's sometimes hard for us in the modern age to think about how religion, and Christianity specifically, could have such an outstanding effect on people, leading them to commit heinous crimes or giving them hope and happiness in times of absolute chaos and destruction. But for many individuals throughout history, Christianity was their one and only truth, and anything outside of that was oppressed.

In *Adam*, the oppression comes from a very different place. The characters live in a society where seemingly all culture (religion, language, literature, politics, art, etc.) has been severely repressed, if not fully erased. Adam is confused and terrified when he starts to learn about certain radical beliefs stemming from Christianity. He doesn't understand how anyone could put blind faith in things that can't be explained and thinks the few individuals who do have lost their minds. To him, they aren't seeing reason. I think this is the same reaction someone from the Middle Ages or even the Renaissance would have to modern society where the majority of people can believe anything they want. To Northern Europeans in the Renaissance like Van Eyck and Van der Weyden, anything outside of Christianity was unfathomable, and many people were shunned and put to death if their views didn't conform, much like the Untouchables are in Adam's world.

Van Eyck and Van der Weyden's representations of Judgement Day, the day prophesied in the Bible where God judges everyone, living and dead, and deems whether they will spend eternity in Heaven or Hell, and the total destruction leading up to the final judgement in Revelation—the destruction that is painted in detail in both of the artist's works—inspired the absolute destruction of the Regime, the society in *Adam* that was thought by its population to be invincible. In Revelation, seven plagues destroy the Earth, bringing war, famine, disease, and what we'd consider natural disasters: violent, deadly earthquakes, wildfires, and floods. This total chaos becomes the massive earthquakes, tsunamis, floods, fires, and volcanic eruption that devastate the Regime in *Adam*.

For individuals like Van Eyck and Van der Weyden who

lived in the 15th century, Revelation was read by nearly everyone. Those who lacked literacy relied on the grueling, painted images of sadism and brutality awaiting those who lived in sin and did not repent, and, on the other hand, the grace to come by those disciples and followers of the Church. Artists generally chose to represent Heaven and Hell as described during the days of judgement on the left and right, respectively. The left represented good, and the right represented evil and the burning depths of Hell containing all those deemed unworthy to be the sons and daughters of the Trinity. In Revelation 21:8, the unworthy are described as the "cowardly, the faithless, the polluted . . . murderers, fornicators, sorcerers, idolaters, and all liars," and are those that "shall be in the lake that burns with fire and Sulphur, which is the second death." Not only did individuals during this time fear dying, they feared the day they'd face a second death—for them, there was no question if Judgement Day would happen; it was a given. Like the descriptions in Revelation, the dark, terrifying images of Judgement Day painted by artists like Van Eyck and Van der Weyden were meant to provoke individuals into repenting their sins and living a holy life.

Between 1445-48, Van der Weyden produced his version of Judgement Day, known as both the *Beaune Altarpiece* and the *Last Judgement* Altarpiece, for a French hospital in Beaune. The painting can now be found in the Musée de l'Hôtel-Dieu in Beaune, France. He painted a pessimistic view of human nature, in which most of the individuals being judged are being pulled almost magnetically toward Hell, depicted as a black, fiery waste, and very few are allowed to enter the golden cathedral that represents Heaven.

Most representations of Judgement Day did not leave the fate of humanity up to humans, but angels and demons fought one another for the souls of mankind; this is based on the descriptions of the great battle between the Holy and the Evil in Revelation. Van Eyck's *Last Judgement*, which can be seen at the Metropolitan Museum in New York City, exemplifies this.

St. Michael the Archangel is pictured standing in the middle of the painting directly above a winged skeletal figure representing Death, wielding a sword and fighting against Evil for humanity. Many rescued souls are pictured in Heaven, unlike in Van der Weyden's altarpiece, but Van Eyck still chose to represent a gruesome, crowded Hell below the wings of Death. Through extraordinary detail, he demonstrates what many imagined to be the atrocities of the Underworld. Demons, dragons, and serpents eat the flesh off the fallen and weave their way through—literally—the bodies of the damned.

The horrors of Judgement Day that were written about and depicted through works of art like those of Van Eyck and Van Der Weyden have inspired conversations about what the end of the world might look like for thousands of years. As people have done throughout history, Adam and the characters in the Regime tried to find answers to the seemingly inexplicable catastrophe destroying everything they thought they knew, and like people have done and continue to do, Adam and Eve wondered if it was possible that any higher power could have a say in what was happening to their world.

Though it seems like the end of the world in *Adam*, the book serves not as a depiction of a literal Judgement Day, but a commentary on what happens when individuals are faced with situations that are frightening and unprecedented in their minds.

ACKNOWLEDGMENTS

This book wouldn't have been possible without the support of my friends and family. To them, I owe the world! This book has been a long-time coming, and I cannot express how much it means to me that it's in your hands.

The dream to write this started when I was in college in 2016, and it wasn't until after I'd graduated that I really had time to devote to finishing the story. That being said, if it weren't for my mother and sister, who spent long hours with me editing and developing *Adam*, I wouldn't have had the courage to share it with you. I am beyond grateful for their love and support, and please remember that if there's something you want to share with the world, share it! Don't let your fears hold you back.

Shelby Wratchford grew up outside St. Louis, MO, on a hobby farm with her parents and sister, exploring the woods around their home and learning to grow and care for plants and animals. She has a deep love of art history and is interested in the connections between science, religion, philosophy, and literature. You can find her painting the wildlife she sees on her farm, reading science fiction—and some romance, of course—that leaves her wondering what the hell just happened, drinking Manhattans, and contemplating the end of the world. *Adam* is her debut novel. To learn more about Shelby, check out her Instagram: shelby.wratchford.

9 781737 076902